Romance

NO MORE

MISSED

OPPORTUNITIES

Not the kind of person he anticipated seeing at his daughter's wedding.

Spencer Smart

"How are things going, Dad?"

I shook my head and grinned. We were at my daughter Bethany's wedding reception when she asked how I was. Say what you want about my ex and my relationship, but we did very well regarding parenting. Either that, or we were fortunate. It was most likely a combination of the two.

"That's what I'm supposed to ask you." Bethany smiled and kissed me on the cheek in response to my response. She took a step back, and her grin shifted to a scowl, which perplexed me until she reached out and wiped away the lipstick she'd left behind. I couldn't stop myself from taunting her. "You don't need all that makeup, you know. You're stunning even without it."

It was a running joke between us. It dated back to her early adolescence when she was still figuring out how much makeup was too much. We used to get into heated debates over it all the time.

"That's what I'm always telling her." Neil approached and slipped his arm around my daughter's. He had the right now that he was her husband, I suppose. What was I thinking? He was right long before they spoke wedding vows, but only because no one else could make my little girl's eyes sparkle as he could.

Bethany and Neil have that particular spark that sure couples possess. I thought it would help them get through the difficult times, and there will be difficult times. They were present at all weddings. Mine most definitely did. Unfortunately, Bethany's mother, Adrian, and I didn't make it, but to be honest, that spark was never there in our marriage.

Understand me. There was a moment when we were in love with one other. Hell, I believe we still did, just not in that sense. You didn't spend almost twenty-five years together unless it was founded on something genuine. Regrettably, it wasn't always enough.

"I know it would have been your 25th wedding anniversary next week, Dad. You don't have to if Mom having Don with her disturbs you..." Bethany had a knack for predicting my emotions.

"I'm alright," I said, interjecting. "And Don seems to be a kind man. I'm glad for your mum, believe it or not. You can't blame an elderly guy for being sad at his daughter's wedding, but I lost my precious baby to this jerk today." It was a pitiful effort at levity. Neil was kind enough to chuckle. Bethany took a step away from him long enough to embrace me and speak in my ear.

"Don't be a moron! I'll always be your young lady." She stepped back into Neil's arms before saying, "You aren't even that old. You're just 51 years old."

Neil taunted, "You know." "My aunt Ann is not married..."

"Don't even consider it." I didn't want to be set up by his freshly minted son-in-law or anybody else. After all, I'd met his aunt Ann. She was unattached for a reason.

"I'm simply saying that I'm pretty certain you'll strike it rich tonight. You know, ladies and weddings." Neil had a peculiar sense of humor. It was one of the qualities I admired in him; my daughter, on the other hand, did not, at least not, in front of her father.

Bethany smacked Neil on the shoulder, which just made him laugh. I hugged my daughter and kissed her quickly. Of course, Neil, being Neil, couldn't stop there. She took a step away from Bethany and smiled at me before saying, "I could notify Aunt Ann that you are interested. Simply utter the word."

"You do, and my daughter will be a widow before the night's end." The threat was meaningless, but he understood what he was saying. Neil seemed to be about to torment me some more, but he turned behind me and whatever he saw caused him to lose his grin.

"Oh hell," groaned my new son-in-law. "Walt Millerson has arrived. He's one of my company's partners. I didn't want to invite him, but I couldn't invite everyone else if I didn't ask him."

"That must be incredibly annoying now that you're going to give your notice when you return from your honeymoon." My son-in-law was highly accomplished at what he did and swiftly rose the ranks. He hadn't intended on leaving his present work just yet, but he got one of those impossible-to-refuse employment offers from another firm.

"Right?" Neil snorted. "If only I'd known before I sent out the invites." "At least the arm candy with him this time seems more age-appropriate," he muttered, looking over my shoulder again.

"Wow, she's beautiful," my daughter said. I was intrigued, but I didn't think turning around and looking was very lovely.

"They are always." Neil took a deep breath and turned to face my daughter. "Let's hope this one has a mind of its own. The previous one was half his age and had four of his IQ. We can't possibly avoid him forever, I guess."

"Are you certain?" I smiled. "I've spent the whole night avoiding your aunt Ann. So far, everything is going well." That made Neil chuckle once again, which was kind of the idea. Of course, the disadvantage was that it made my daughter moan.

"You know," she sighed deeply. "I'm just now realizing how much you two resemble one other."

"There's no way!" Neil responded. "I'm a lot funnier."

"And more attractive," I simply added. "However, this is mere because you are younger. After all, I'm still smarter."

"Do you mean just because I'm younger?"

Some people were astonished by my friendship with Neil, but the fact was that I'd known him since he was ten years old and moved in next door. His father was a kind man, although he worked a lot and was a little geeky. Neil learned how to play baseball from me. I'd taught him many things over the years, after all. On the other hand, I also learned a lot from him. My kid might have fared far worse.

"You should have seen me when I was younger," I joked. "I was very darn attractive." I'm sure my son-in-law was prepared with a solid retort, but this man Walt took advantage of the situation to locate Neil and my daughter.

"Neil! My son!" As he interrupted our talk, the guy stated. He attempted to shove me aside, which was amusing in its own right. Of course, I had to reach out and place my hand on Bethany's arm to calm her down since she wasn't amused. I felt she was being a little dramatic, but it was her wedding day, and emotions ran high. "And this must be your gorgeous wife!" he said, seemingly obliviously.

He raised his arms as if expecting an embrace from my daughter. Bethany, on the other hand, took a step closer to me. To be honest, I didn't blame her. He gave off a sinister sense.

"My name is Bethany," she answered, frowning. "And here's my father." I took a step forward, partly to shake his hand and partially to place myself between him and my daughter, which was ridiculous, but as she had stated earlier, she would always be my little girl, and Bethany didn't like Walt.

The person genuinely looked at me with disgust, which was unusual given that we'd never met before. Walt certainly never had a shot with Bethany, but he wasn't making things easier for himself.

"My name is John." I extended my hand, assuming it was my responsibility to preserve the peace.

"Ah yeah, the guy who thinks he's 'pretty darn good looking,'" Walt commented as he grudgingly grasped my hand and shook it.

So, not only did this person try to push me aside, but he also chose to pass judgment on me based on a portion of a discussion he'd been impolite enough to interrupt. Earlier, he mistook my seriousness for jest. I couldn't help myself. I burst out laughing.

"When I was younger," I explained, still amused. I'd concluded that this was too important a day to allow someone like Walt to destroy. Years from now, he'd be just a humorous tale.

"You haven't changed that much."

The voice was coming from behind me. Even though I hadn't heard it in over twenty-five years, I instantly knew it had a mocking tone. Was it even possible? Could you recall a voice after such a long time? The answer seemed simple, yet a part of me was still unsure.

"This is my date, Jessica," Walt added, deepening his scowl as he pointed behind me. I imagine he didn't like how she'd decided to participate in the discourse. After twenty-five years, I looked around, and there she was.

"Hey Johnny," she said as I took in her beauty. I wasn't shocked to find that she was still in terrific shape. Jessica had always been the sort to look after herself. Nonetheless, the years appeared to have only enhanced her attractiveness. Her hair was as long and black as I recalled. Her eyes were much more enticing than I remembered.

Don't get me wrong: Jessica seemed to be her age, but she was the sexiest fifty-year-old I'd ever seen. That's when I realized my kid was gazing at me strangely. I shook my head and smiled back at my first serious girlfriend.

"Hey, Jess, it's been a while." Yes, I know, but that was the best I could come up with, given how startled I was to see her at my daughter's wedding. Okay, there was a little more than that. My response to seeing Jessica was what truly jolted me. After all these years, how could she still make me feel this way?

She walked into me and quickly hugged me, as old friends are known to do. I gripped her for a moment, feeling pieces of myself awaken that I thought were long dead. Just the fragrance of her reminded me of how we used to be.

"I see you're still wearing the same scent," I murmured, hoping no one saw how unsteady I was. Jessica smiled and shook her head, but she didn't say anything. It was a long-running joke between us. But then, everything between us was old news. I felt remorse, but then I saw Bethany, and it vanished. Things occurred the way they did for a reason.

"Jessica doesn't wear perfume," Walt grumbled, drawing my attention back to Jessie. "She has an allergy."

"I know," I chuckled, not knowing what else to say. Walt seems perplexed and unimpressed. Jessica didn't bother responding, despite a slight flush. Bethany, on the other hand, had a few words. Fortunately, her maid of honor stopped us before my daughter could say anything.

"Sorry for bothering you, but they're on the dance floor searching for you both. It's time for the bride and groom to dance."

"That's our signal." Okay, so I was happy to get away from the talk with the look in my daughter's eyes, but I was also having difficulty walking away from Jessie... again. When I looked at her, I knew she understood precisely what I was thinking. I couldn't let it go at that. "Perhaps we can catch up later?"

"We're not staying that long," Walt said, evidently dissatisfied with the apparent bond between his companion and me. When I glanced at Jessica, she shrugged and grinned. Damn.

"Well, it was wonderful seeing you again, Jess," I replied, leaning in for one more embrace. "Look after yourself."

"And you, Johnny." Jessica shocked me by kissing the inside of my cheek. Then it was her time to wipe her lipstick off my face. Despiteough the motion was identical, the impact on me was much different than when from

The bandleader had summoned my daughter and me to the dance floor. I smiled at Jessica and moved my gaze to my kid. I refused to look her in the eyes and took her to the dance floor. The band began performing 'Butterfly Kisses.' Yeah, I realize it's not that inventive, but so what? Some things didn't have to be that way.

"What was it all about?" my daughter inquired as I cradled her in my arms and began dancing. I arched an eyebrow at her and looked her in the eyes.

"Are you sure you want to ask that now?" Bethany looked at me for a little more before softly chuckling.

"No, but don't believe it's the end. There's a tale there, which you'll tell me."

I shook my head as I glanced at my kid. At times, she sounded frighteningly similar to her mother, but that wasn't necessarily negative. Of course, it didn't mean I wasn't going to tell her about Jessica later.

Jess was from my past, and she had come to see me. Okay, so I could have thought about her throughout the years, particularly now that I was divorced, but we didn't have anything in common except for some attraction that I couldn't understand after all these years.

"I still can't believe I'm a married woman." As she shifted the topic, my daughter smiled.

"You?" I laughed and snorted. "I still believe you're a young girl half the time, as the song says." I took a hiatus and shook my head. When the music reached the chorus, I couldn't help but sing quietly to her.

"...stuck small white flowers all over her hair..."

"Please, don't!" Bethany exclaimed. "I'm going to lose it if you do!"

"Even if I sing so badly?" I taunted her, hoping to get her to laugh. It was just another tired joke. It seemed to be their night.

"Especially with that!" she exclaimed, and we both laughed. That didn't stop her eyes from watering. Mine wasn't much better.

The remainder of the dance went by in a haze. Bethany needed to stretch her wings and start her own family. I was so proud of the beautiful lady my daughter had grown into, but I knew a part of me would always mourn the little girl she'd been. I couldn't stop joining in and singing the song's ending.

"...With all I've done wrong, there must be something I've done well! To be worthy of your love every morning and butterfly kisses—I couldn't ask God for anything more, buddy; this is what love is! I know I have to let her go, but I'll remember embrace and butterfly kiss."

"I despise you!" Bethany snapped as a few tears streamed down her face, but then she leaned in and kissed me with moist butterfly kisses to soothe the pain of her words.

"I love you, too, baby-girl," I said, tears threatening to fall as I kissed her. Bethany smiled briefly before turning and exiting the dance floor. I let her go since she was going toward Neil, standing with my ex. Adrian and I were on good terms, considering, but I was too distraught to face her and her boyfriend at the time.

I'm not sure whether it was seeing Jess, dealing with Adrian and her boyfriend, dancing with Bethany, or simply because it was my daughter's wedding day, but I was feeling down.

I hadn't experienced the life I had envisioned for myself as a young man. At this stage, I expected to have many essentially grown-up children, a lady next to me who was my better half, and a feeling of... something... maybe completeness?

On the other hand, Bethany had turned out even better than I had hoped. A better daughter could not be imagined for a parent. She was the source of my pride and delight. I knew I wasn't going to lose her. Not in any critical way, but things would be different today.

"You're glad Dad isn't here." When I turned to face the speaker, I noticed my brother Tommy grinning. "No son of his would dare to disgrace him in public by sobbing."

"You're right, big brother," I chuckled, relieved by Tommy's interruption. "However, I recall someone blubbering like a child at his daughter's wedding last year."

"I didn't burst out laughing! It was a single tear, and something was in my eye. "He was confident.

"You just keep telling yourself that," his wife Emily chided as she came over to join us.

"Hey, I wasn't even half as awful as him!"

"Perhaps not," I conceded. "However, you still have a single daughter. Wait until you're saying your final farewell."

Tommy moaned, "Ouch." "I'm not even going to think about it."

We exited the dance floor because Neil needed to dance with his mother. Mary, our younger sister, joined us. She was holding an additional drink, which she gave me right away.

"Thank you," I responded as I took it and downed half of it in one gulp. "That was what I needed. You've saved my life."

"So," my sister said, without further ado. Her grin told me I was in for a treat. "Did I just glimpse a ghost?"

There was no need to specify who she was referring to. There was only one person who could elicit the kind of emotion my sister did.

"Yes, Jessica has arrived."

"There's no way!" Tommy burst out crying before I could explain what had occurred. "No, you didn't!"

"Are you insane?" In reaction, I snapped. "Don't be a moron! I didn't invite her, of course. I haven't seen Jess in more years than I want to remember."

"So, what brings her here?" Mary shook her head as if she didn't believe me.

"Would you think she's here as one of Neil's bosses' dates?" It was only now that the impossibility of it all began to dawn on me.

"Did you two talk?" Emily was smiling in a manner that bothered me. When she was in a foul mood, she could be just as terrible as Mary.

"Briefly," I answered simply.

"With you two, it would be enough." Emily was a complete jerk. "I have a feeling this will be a fascinating night."

"Look," I groaned, wanting to reach out to my siblings. They may be challenging at times, particularly with something like this. "Jess is here with a date, and now isn't the moment, even if I was interested in her."

"Please," Mary said, snorting. "You've always had a thing for Jessie 'that way.'"

"So not the point," I grumbled, not trying to refute it before looking them all in the eyes. "At the end of the day, this is Bethany's wedding, and I don't want anything to detract from that."

"I believe you're referring to detract, little brother." Tommy was speaking in the tone of an older brother, which he knew I despised. He, too, was beaming. I shook my head and thought about what I'd just said.

"I don't want anything to take away from, distract from, or otherwise disrupt Bethany's special day." I took a hiatus to ensure they knew I was serious. "You'll forget you met Jess tonight. Tomorrow you may torment me all you want, but today is all about Bethany."

"That's all right." Emily was always the most considerate of the four of us. As the other two nodded in agreement, I nearly sighed a sigh of relief, but then my sister had to wreck it.

"However, you'd best hope Adrian doesn't notice her." The wide-eyed look on Mary's face told it all. "Whether she does or not, the fireworks will be tremendous."

"You got it correct," Tommy pointed out.

"I think I need another drink." I'd already completed the one my sister had given me.

"I'm not convinced getting drunk is the best way to deal with this circumstance." Emily was frowning, and I could tell what she was saying. Even so, I needed at least one more drink.

"I'm not convinced there's a good solution to this problem. Maybe all he can do is get drunk." Tommy and his wife began to argue. I shook my head and looked across at Mary. We exchanged a fleeting grin over their heads as she rolled her eyes.

"I should probably go locate my date." Tommy and Emily didn't seem to notice my sister's remark. Mary arrived with an unknown man. I say random because I knew she wasn't interested in him. If she were, I would have met him earlier than tonight. "I'll see you in a minute." My younger sister walked away from us, and I returned my attention to my elder brother and sister-in-law.

Tommy and Emily battled often, but it never amounted to anything. They were virtually always fine when a fight was over. I was constantly envious of them because of it. Adrian and I used to quarrel all the time, and it never turned out half as well for us. To be honest, I frequently ended up sleeping in the spare bedroom. By the time I moved out, most of my belongings were there.

I barely stayed for a few seconds before leaving them to their strange form of foreplay. At least, that's what I used to taunt them about when they were disputing. They never denied it.

I went to one of the two bars and ordered a new drink. It was just my luck that Walt picked the same one. When he spotted me, he grimaced. I tried to ignore him since I was not in the mood to talk to him again, but he had something to say.

"So, how do you know Jessica?" he questioned flatly. I was perplexed as to why he wasn't asking her that question. Something about this man bothered me, and it had nothing to do with the fact that he was here with Jess.

"Old pals," I said concisely, thinking he'd get the idea and move on, but Walt wasn't the sort to take a hint.

"Well, don't get any ideas," he replied, giving me what I'm sure he thought was an ominous look. I nearly burst out laughing. I was too old for this nonsense.

Walt was as well, but it didn't appear to disturb him. "It took me three months to get her to go on a date with me, and you're not going to spoil that."

I didn't bother to respond. Instead, I accepted the drink the bartender had delivered and placed a tip in his jar. I started to walk away, but Walt dared to grasp my arm. I returned my attention to him and raised an eyebrow.

I would have reacted differently if I were a younger guy. Even if it hadn't been my daughter's wedding, I might have gone anyhow. He was fortunate I wasn't intoxicated yet. At least he was wise enough to see something in my look because he quickly released go of my arm.

"I'd want to say it's been a joy, Walt, but it hasn't been." I'd had enough of being polite to this man.

"Remember, Jessica came with me and was going with me. I've worked far too long and hard to let someone like you derail my ambitions."

"I mean, it's been a long time since I've seen Jess, but I wouldn't get my hopes up if I were you. She has a greater sense of style than you."

"Yet she is here with me." It was a reasonable assertion. Why was Jess such a jerk? So, girl, I recalled, couldn't possibly be that desperate. Perhaps the reason was that, despite the desire, I still felt for her; Jessica wasn't the same girl I remembered from my childhood.

I turned and left Walt, primarily because there was nothing more for us to say to one other, and there was a strong possibility he was correct. Jess and I just had the past. I wasn't going to delude myself into believing there was anything more between us than that, especially not tonight. Maybe I'd feel differently in the morning, but maybe not.

The following couple of hours passed fast. I made my way around the tables, greeting everyone. I knew individuals on both sides since I'd met Neil's family many times. I loved the majority of them, particularly his parents. They were decent individuals.

I did see Jess a few times, but Walt was always at her side, and as I told my sister, I didn't want any drama during Bethany's wedding, so I ignored them. Before I knew it, the bride and groom were cutting the cake.

Mary, Tommy, and Emily stood beside me as I watched Bethany and Neil perform the ceremony. When they were finished, my brother whacked me on the shoulder.

"Almost there," he said, smiling. I shook my head but appreciated his support. I enjoyed them all being there for me. I was fortunate to have such a family.

"Are we still getting together for brunch on Sunday?" Emily inquired, evidently attempting to divert my attention away from my sadness, but the fact was that I was okay. I was overjoyed for my daughter.

Mary, on the other hand, was not nearly as helpful. She didn't even give me a chance to respond to our sister-in-query law before asking, "Have you had a chance to speak with Jessie?"

"Seriously?" I let my displeasure show, but my younger sister disregarded my pointed glare while stating unequivocally that she wouldn't let the subject go until she had an answer. I sighed and mainly surrendered because Jess had been on my mind for the whole night, despite my best attempts to ignore her presence and enjoy the wedding. "Would you believe her date had warned me earlier at the bar? Plus, he hasn't abandoned her."

"Please let us know if you wish to speak with her. We can look after him." I was taken aback when Emily made the proposition. Since their sophomore year of high school, I'd known my sister-in-law when she and Tommy began dating. In our family, she was usually the voice of reason.

Here's the strange part: I was pretty tempted to accept her offer. I was buzzed enough to acknowledge that I wanted to talk to Jess again, but this wasn't the time. When we were ready to inform my siblings about it, we were stopped.

"Wow, this is a terrifying sight." And there it was once again. That tone of voice. My heart rate increased. "Someone will not be pleased to see all four of you together. I'm hoping it's not me."

"Not you," Mary responded, widening her grin as Jess approached. "It's your date."

"Please, please! Whatever you have planned, make it happen as quickly as possible, "Jessica sighed. "I've had about as much as I can take of him."

"Hey, you promised to accompany him," Tommy pointed out.

"Please don't remind me."

"Nice to meet you, Jessie." Jessica hugged Emily as she had her arms extended. Mary quickly followed suit. Tommy, too, embraced her quickly.

Walt came over to join us at that time, but my siblings, being what they were, disregarded him. Me, too, but mainly because I was terrified, I'd become too intoxicated and do something dumb.

"I still can't believe you married this loser," Jess said to Emily, reverting to the mocking she'd had with my family years before.

"She had no choice," my brother said solemnly. He wasn't deceiving anybody. "I beat her up." His wife smacked him on the back of the shoulder for it.

"I may have given birth to our first child just eight months after our wedding, but we were engaged a year before that," she snarled. "And you were supposed to make sure we didn't become pregnant before the wedding."

"Oops." My brother's smile earned him another, heavier hit from his wife. "Oh, please! We weren't planning on having children immediately quickly, after all."

"Were you pregnant during your wedding?" This from Walt, who appeared to become dumber and dumber with each opening of his lips. His displeasure in his speech was a tremendous blunder for my family. We may have continually picked on one other, but that was our style. No one from the outside was going to say anything about our family.

We all turned and confronted him at the same time. I wasn't surprised that Walt took a step back when he saw our unified front, but I was astonished to see Jess standing with us, staring at him with the same disgusted face.

"Aha! I had a feeling there was more to you two. "My daughter sobbed, and she and Neil joined us, maybe sparing Walt's life or at the very least his dignity. Bethany shifted her gaze to Jessica. "Can you tell me your name?"

"Well, if things had turned out differently," my brother started. I attempted to cut him off because I was worried I knew where he was headed, but Tommy, being Tommy, there was no stopping him once he began, mainly when he was ready to stick his foot in his mouth. "She could've been your mother." Mary and I both moaned out as we both winced.

"Smooth," his wife said with a sigh.

"What? That is the truth." For a few seconds, there was an awkward quiet.

"I'm satisfied with the mother I have, thank you very much," Bethany stated tersely to her uncle before turning her attention to Jessica and slowly adding, "But that doesn't mean I'm not aware my father is responding. To you."

"Reacting?" I inquired, but all I received were frowns and eye rolls from my family.

Neil snorted, "Give it up." "You're almost sadistic in your love for her."

"I don't like where this debate is headed," Walt remarked, but my family ignored him once again.

"Me, too," I whispered, but no one was paying attention to me.

"Wait, Jessica?" my daughter said, her eyes widening. "Is this Jezebel?" Bethany said, turning toward me. I sighed. There was no way this was going to work.

"Jezebel?" With a grimace, Jess inquired.

"Mom constantly referred to Dad's first love in this manner. Are you sure you're here?" My kid didn't appear bothered by what she was asking. In contrast, I was humiliated.

"I am not a Jezebel," Jess said simply, but then added, "Although, I'm quite sure I am your father's first love and based on the last discussion your mother and I had, Jezebel was probably the nicest word she ever called me." That was insufficient for Bethany. She moved her gaze to me and waited patiently.

"You understand I'm a fifty-one-year-old guy," I pointed out. That didn't make Bethany feel any better, so I added, "And your father." That calmed my daughter down. Unfortunately, she wasn't the only one in the room.

Tommy shrugged, "It's not like it's a secret." "Everyone is aware that Jess was your first."

"My first love," I explained, my blushing even more.

"That, too!" said my elder brother. That drew a third slap from his wife and an elbow from Mary. The latter was located in the stomach. It wasn't difficult, but it did eventually silence Tommy. Jess shook her head, but she didn't look as ashamed as me. I believe she was a little tipsy herself. I couldn't say I blamed her. I'd be exhausted entirely if I had to deal with someone like Walt all evening, much alone my family.

"Everything about this circumstance is priceless!" Neil replied, not even attempting to conceal his delight at my expense.

"The only way it could be more intriguing is if Mom finds out you're here." Bethany seems amused by the incident. I'm sure she wasn't anticipating this on her wedding day. I certainly wasn't.

"Oh, I see," Jess said. "That's why I've been hiding in the background and avoiding her all night, but when I saw them all together, I couldn't pass up the opportunity to say hello."

"I don't blame you for hiding," Neil laughed as he reached out and took my daughter's hand in his. "Bethany's mother can be a frightening person." I was pretty sure that would elicit a response. I wasn't mistaken.

"I'm not frightened of her," Jessica said emphatically. "There was a period when I felt for her very much the same way she feels about me, but I determined long ago that holding on to those sentiments was too much like being a disgruntled loser."

"Did you despise Adrian?" I inquired, surprised. I understood how my ex felt about Jessica, but I had no idea it was reciprocal.

Okay, it was strange to watch my kid and Jess share a glance and then roll their eyes in tandem, particularly given they'd just met a few minutes before.

"Men," shrugged my daughter. Fortunately, my son-in-law came to my aid.

"So, if you're not terrified of Bethany's mother and no longer despise her, why are you avoiding her?" Neil inquired.

"It's her daughter's wedding," Jess said, shrugging. "I don't want to sour her mood."

"However, here you are." A voice from behind me startled me again. Only this one I was familiar with. Adrian. Oh, no. This was not going to end well. I shifted my gaze.

I didn't precisely moan when my ex-wife appeared. As if things weren't already weird. At the very least, Adrian was not accompanied by Don. My whole family, including Tommy and Neil, became quiet for the first time all night.

"As my date," Walt chimed in. I had completely forgotten he was here.

Adrian snorted with astonishment, "Keep telling yourself that." "But I'm guessing she only consented to accompany you once you told her the bride's name."

The charge seemed a little far-fetched. I was surprised Jessica didn't refute it right away. The grimace on Walt's face astonished me even more. Is it possible?

"Look, I'm not wanting to create any issues," Jess said Adrian in one of the strangest times of my life. "I'm going to leave." My ex-wife, I was sure, would instruct her to do just that, but Adrian shook her head.

"No," my ex said hesitantly. "When I told John that I wanted to invite Don to the wedding, he was quite accommodating. He might have made things unpleasant for himself." Adrian was being a lot more reasonable than I had anticipated. Don was probably excellent for her. "After all, he didn't bring you." She paused before saying, "In any case, the reception is nearly finished. Please do me a favor and refrain from using PDAs tonight." And with that, my ex vanished. To be honest, I was dumbfounded.

"She's my date," Walt said again, sounding irritated and whiney. I didn't think much of Walt, but I couldn't resist giving him this one. He had every right to be upset. I might have felt awful if he had been more like. It wouldn't have prevented what occurred next, but it would have made it less straightforward. It was time for Walt to depart, and I was more than willing to tell him so.

"The reception is over for you," Neil said with a grin before finishing my sentence. "And it seems that your date is as well."

"However," Walt started.

"Thank you for bringing me Walt," Jess remarked cheerfully. "I'll figure out how to go home on my own."

I moved between Jess and him since he was obviously about to say something hurtful. That drew his attention to me, which was good. I didn't care what he said about myself, but if he said anything about Jess, I could have gotten into a fight. What was I thinking? I most certainly would have.

"Have you met my aunt Ann, Walt?" Neil stepped in, grabbed the guy's arm, and practically dragged him away. "She's a real beauty."

"You know, I almost feel terrible for Neil's aunt," I murmured, shaking my head after they'd left. "She's not my favorite person, but I'm not convinced she deserves Walt."

"What a jerk," my daughter said.

"You're not incorrect," Jessica remarked with a sigh of disdain. "You have no idea how relieved I was when I came and saw that you were Johnny's daughter. I mean, how many ladies with the surname Bethany could there be? Even still, if I'd been mistaken, I'd have been trapped with Walt all night for no apparent reason."

"So, Mom was correct," my daughter murmured, her gaze fixed on Jessica. "You've come because you wanted to visit my father."

"Whatever I may have said in the past about your mother," Jess shrugged. "It was never the case that she was foolish." Jessica took a short pause before saying, "It wasn't only your father either. I'm just a year younger than him, and my birthday was just a few weeks ago. It was a huge one, so I spent a lot of time reflecting on my life. I was also wondering how your aunts and uncle were doing. Don't overlook it. They were my neighbors when I was a kid. Of course, if I hadn't heard your parents were divorcing, I would not have come." Her arguments were rational and, I'm sure, truthful, but my daughter was much too intelligent to be distracted by them.

"You're still madly in love with your father." It wasn't a question, and it humiliated me.

"Are you in love?" Jess averted her gaze for the first time, uneasy with the topic. "Perhaps once, but it was a long time ago. That was not the reason I came here."

"Sure, it's not," my younger sister sniffed, amused. "How about you tell the truth?"

"Are you aware I'm standing right here?" I felt that was a reasonable inquiry.

"Yes, now shut up," Tommy said with a grin. "I'd want to hear her response." "Well, do you still love him?" my brother questioned, turning toward Jess in his straightforward style. She didn't respond right away.

Jessica's deep brown eyes were locked on mine, and I could feel my heartbeat speeding. "I don't know about love," she said softly. "However, there does seem to be something between us." She halted, her gaze fixed on mine. "To be honest, it's a little stronger than I anticipated."

"Just a little," Emily said.

"However, in the end, it doesn't matter." Jess opted to disregard my sister-in-remark's law as she pushed ahead, eventually looking away from me. "What we had was too long ago to reignite even if we wanted to, and to be honest, I'm not sure I want to. It was excruciating and ended poorly. Why would I want to go through it again?"

"If I were in your situation, I'd feel the same way," my sister said with a grin. "But there are two things you should consider before making your decision. First and foremost, you've arrived." I expected my sister to emphasize the significance of that information further, but she looked like Jess and felt she'd made her point. "Second, Johnny isn't the same guy he was back then. I'm guessing neither do you. Don't allow former versions of yourself to ruin the present."

"I've changed," Jess responded, shaking her head. "That is precisely my point. We can't go back in time."

"No, we can't," I reluctantly agreed. It was true, and I couldn't argue with her, but the final thing my sister said was more significant, at least to me, and hopefully to Jess as well. "But that doesn't mean we can't catch up and re-acquaint ourselves. That's something I'd want." I saw my daughter nod to herself as her aunts and uncle laughed and grinned, but I ignored them and concentrated on Jess. There was a lengthy pause.

"Okay," Bethany murmured into the ensuing stillness. "Just keep in mind what Mom said. There will be no public demonstrations of love."

"You don't have to be concerned," Jessica remarked, shaking her head. "Tonight, or any other time for that matter. The chances of your father and I reuniting after all this time..."

"Are very excellent," Mary chimed in. "If any of you feel like making a friendly wager..."

"You are not assisting," my sister-in-law groaned but immediately changed into a smile as she added, "However if you find a sucker to accept that bet, let me know." I'll join in with you." Emily has known my brother for far too long. At moments, she sounded just like him.

"I wouldn't be so sure," Jessica said, shaking her head. She was chatting with everyone, but she was talking to me. "Johnny vanished and got engaged to someone else the last time we talked. I still haven't forgiven him."

"That's up to you two to figure out... or not." My daughter was wise enough to see that it was time for her to go. "But I must say that it was a pleasure to meet you. I'd always wondered how you were." Jessica eventually turned away from me and turned to face my kid.

"Nice meeting you as well," Jessica said with a grin. "And best wishes on your wedding." My daughter thanked me and then walked away.

"I suppose I should go find my date again," my sister said, sighing. "Hopefully, he beat Walt to Neil's aunt Ann's house, and they're on their way someplace."

"Is it that bad?" The question was rhetorical. I'd already met her date. He was merely the latest in a long series of losers. Mary was intelligent, humorous, and gorgeous. Unfortunately, she had poor taste in guys. I couldn't even recall the name of this one.

"You had a good concept. I should've come as a stag." I knew Mary was serious since I had grown up with her.

"Things might be a lot worse." Jess still had that teasing smile I remembered so well despite the years. "You could have accompanied Walt."

"But look how it worked out for you," my sister remarked.

"Only time will tell." Jess' tone was reserved. It made me think of how obstinate she could be at times.

I wasn't as sure as my sister that things would work out between Jess and myself. Sure, our most recent breakup was all my fault, but it wasn't the first time we had a falling out. There was a lot of history between us that none of them knew about.

"We'll talk afterward." Mary was saying goodbye to everyone, but she was gazing at me to indicate she'd be calling for all the specifics in the morning.

"Don't be a stranger," Emily remarked warmly to Jessica as she and my brother prepared to depart. "I understand why we couldn't remain close back then, but we've always been friends, and there should be no reason we can't reconnect again, even if you two don't work out," my sister-in-law said as she leaned in hugged Jess.

"That's something I'd want." When I heard Jess's voice, I was taken aback. It was rich with abrupt emotion, and her eyes became a bit moist for a split second. "Please forgive me. I believe I had a bit too much to drink. I'm feeling too emotional right now."

I knew Jess and Emily were friends when we were younger, but I had no idea that the significant reason they split away was because of me. In some ways, it made sense. I felt horrible, but there was nothing I could do about it at the time. I'd learned a long time ago not to meditate on the past. It was easier some days than others.

"Yeah, that's because of the booze." My brother's remark was a little sarcastic. We all choose to disregard it. Ignoring one other's mocking was a survival mechanism in my family. Tommy said his goodbyes, and then he and Emily left Jess and me alone. We remained quiet for a few seconds, staring at one other.

"Okay, so this is a little odd."

Jess was correct, and I searched my brain for anything to reply. It should have been simple, but as it turned out, it wasn't. It was probably because we were alone for the first time. The DJ came to my rescue a few moments later. He played a slow tune.

"Let's go dancing."

"Are you certain Adrian wouldn't see it as a PDA?" I couldn't tell whether Jess was serious, having a good time at my expense, or procrastinating.

"I'm prepared to take a risk." For the first time all night, I took off my jacket and tossed it on the back of a nearby chair before grabbing her hand and dragging Jess onto the dance floor. She sprang into my arms readily.

We moved as though the years since our last dance were nothing. I enjoyed having Jess in my arms. That was never a problem for us. The link between us remained. There was more to it than that. It was visceral and genuine. The longer we danced, the more evident this became.

The music changed, but we remained on the dance floor, going from song to song, each one making it more difficult for me to keep my hands to myself. Jess seemed to know exactly what she was doing to me and enjoyed it nearly as much as I did.

Fortunately, the final song stopped, and the wedding ended before I did anything crazy. Not foolish, but certainly against the 'no PDA' rule.

"I haven't danced that much in a long time, and I can't believe it was at your daughter's wedding with you." Jess sounded more than a little taken aback.

"You?" I laughed and snorted. "I used to feel like an old geezer, but I feel better now than in years. Simply being here with you is like sipping from the spring of youth."

"You're simply horny," she chuckled, astounded. I hadn't forgotten how direct Jess could be, but it would take some getting used to.

"Well, absolutely," I confessed. "But it's also your fault." Jess rolled her eyes the way I recalled her doing. It was a strange combination of frustration and delight. It always made me laugh.

"That's when I'll depart. It's good to see you again, Johnny." The notion of her departing nearly wrecked my excellent mood, but then I recalled something.

"You're going to need a ride home." It was a statement rather than a question.

"I'm sure I can Uber it." Jess has always been a tenacious young lady.

"Don't be foolish," I said, probably too vehemently. I pushed myself to calm down, or at least seem calmer, as she raised an eyebrow. "I'll pick you up and take you home. As I previously said, I'd appreciate the opportunity to catch up." Jess remained silent. "Please allow me a few minutes to finish up here."

Again, there was no reaction. I wasn't sure whether her quiet indicated agreement, uncertainty, or that she just didn't want to discuss it anymore and would leave the minute I turned my back.

"Please wait for me." I turned to go but couldn't stop myself from saying, in my best Liam Neeson voice, "If you don't, I will seek you, find you, and murder you." It was a foolish thing to say, and his accent was terrible. I can only attribute it to nervousness. Fortunately, Jess's reply did not disappoint.

"Best wishes." The good news was that her reaction indicated that she understood the movie allusion and was not alarmed by the threat. That plus, she had a rather seductive Eastern European accent. The bad news was that her reaction did not seem to be an agreement to remain.

"I'm serious," I began, but paused, smiled, and explained. "It's not so much the killing as searching and finding." She finally cracked a grin.

"I can't believe you're still quoting movies." Jess seemed to be amused, which was a positive indication.

"I can't believe you're still getting referrals," I responded.

"At the very least, it's not from The Godfather." That made me giggle and brought back some pleasant memories.

"What? You want me to make you an offer you won't be able to refuse'?"

"There it is," she murmured, sounding annoyed but amused. We exchanged a quick chuckle.

" I quit reciting movies a long time ago," I said afterward. "I think it's because you bring it out in me."

"I'm lucky." I shook my head and almost burst out laughing at her monotonous delivery. The last thing I wanted to do was terminate our discussion right now, but the wedding had ended, and I had guests to see off.

"Look, there are a few things I need to complete before going. Could you please wait?" I saw her waffling, which was not exactly what I had hoped for but was much better than anticipated. "Allow me to give you a ride home. On the way home, we may stop for coffee and dessert. We must communicate."

"Are you insane? I may not be able to eat for a week after this wedding! After all, it's much too late for coffee." Despite her comments, the twinkle in her eyes gave me hope.

"All right, then, just a ride home." I looked her in the eyes, hoping she'd accept my offer, but Jess was a stubborn girl, as I'd said before.

"I live more than an hour away."

"Perfect! This will give us enough time to catch up. I'm eager to learn more about you and your life." I paused, urgently trying to think of anything that would entice her to accept my offer. "I'm sure you'd want to do the same. After all, you came to the wedding thinking Bethany was my daughter."

"Perhaps I've already learned everything there is to know."

Neither of us believed it, but the issue was, how could I persuade her? I decided to take a risk. I moved up close to Jess and snatched a kiss. Her expression was priceless, but she didn't back down.

I immediately realized that the kiss had been a mistake, but not because it had frightened her away. Jess responded to my kiss with unexpected intensity. Since the first time we met each other, the sparks flying between us had grown into a full-fledged fire. I'd call it a damned inferno, but it wasn't the time or place for that.

"So much for your vow to refrain from using PDAs." Thankfully, the voice that stopped us this time was that of my son-in-law Neil, rather than my daughter's or, worse, my ex-wife's. I drew back hesitantly.

"I never promised, and even if I had, certain things are irreversible."

"You didn't seem to be trying especially hard." Neil appeared more amused than anything else, but he was also apprehensive about how Bethany might take what occurred if she witnessed.

"You make a good argument," I conceded hesitantly. I had no regrets about the kiss. I couldn't, but I didn't want to irritate my kid or my ex.

"Bethany is seeking you," Neil remarked, dropping the topic.

"I'll be right there..."

"That was nasty fighting." Jess had recovered from the kiss and was staring at me, ignoring Neil. I could tell she was furious right now, but it wasn't the only emotion she was experiencing.

"You didn't give me much choice," I shrugged, still not feeling especially bad about the kiss. "I'll be right back. You are free to shout at me while I drive you home." I knew Jess might as well, but I didn't mind as long as she was beside me.

I hadn't felt this life in a long time, and there was no way this was the end of us. That was a mistake I'd made before. Never, ever again.

"You'd be better off waiting. It will be far less expensive than hailing a cab, "Neil chimed in, glancing at me as he spoke to Jessica. "Plus, he'll come up on your doorstep regardless. He's not going to let whatever this is going away." Finally, he turned to Jess and said, "I recognize that expression in his eyes. It's something I've seen before."

"Me, too," Jess acknowledged, not sounding especially pleased. "However, I wasn't anticipating this." She hesitated again before saying gently, "I'm not ready for this."

"Sure you are," I countered. "You're just terrified. I'm afraid, too, but I'm not letting it control me. No, not this time." That piqued her attention, but now wasn't the time to elaborate.

"I need to go back to Bethany," Neil said, realizing it was time for him to go. "I'll delay as long as I can," he said, "but people are hunting for you." As he walked away, I nodded in appreciation and understanding.

"Here," I responded, startling Jess by handing her the keys to my vehicle. "Keep them in mind. You are welcome to drive my vehicle home. We can chat when you get it back." I took a hiatus before continuing, "You may also wait, and I'll give you a ride. It's all up to you. I'm OK with any decision you choose as long as we see each other again."

I turned and walked away before Jess could reclaim my keys. I also silently prayed that I wouldn't find her gone and my keys on the table when I returned.

The most challenging aspect was that saying goodbye and settling everything took much longer than I thought. Bethany and Neil departed for their hotel shortly as I arrived. Adrian and Don vanished immediately, while others took much longer. For a time, my siblings assisted me in ushering the last of the visitors to the door before they said their goodbyes.

Jess had left by the time I returned, but my keys were no longer on the table. Wasn't that a positive sign?

The funny thing was that my tux jacket had vanished as well. I couldn't seem to locate it anyplace. I hoped someone would mistake it for one of the groomsmen's and steal it. We all leased from the exact location, so there shouldn't be a problem as long as they returned it.

Worst case scenario, I'd have to pay for it. It wouldn't be cheap, but nothing else about the wedding had been. On the other side, everything appeared to go swimmingly. More importantly, Bethany was pleased with the outcomes.

As I went out of the reception hall, I took out my phone to schedule an Uber pickup. That's when I happened to run into my brother.

"You're right there!" Tommy screamed, irritated.

"What are you doing still here?" I didn't bother attempting to hide my astonishment in my tone of speech. Instead of responding, he pointed to a bench off to one side with his thumb. Emily was seated next to Jess, dressed in my tux jacket.

"Wipe that shite-eating smile off your face!" yelled my brother. "I'm exhausted, but Emily wouldn't leave Jess alone."

"I owe your wife so much."

"Her?" My brother screamed in frustration. "And how about me?" I ignored him and went straight to the ladies.

"There you have it," Emily spoke the same thing her husband had said before, but without displeasure.

"I apologize for taking longer than intended." I was speaking to all of them while glancing at Jess.

"Can we leave now? I'm exhausted." My brother was being unusually whiny, which was unusual for him.

Emily snorted, clearly amused, "Please." "You're tired has nothing to do with feeling."

"Oh," I said, suddenly understanding. "Is Tommy Jr. staying with Emily's folks tonight?" My brother was the father of three children. One daughter was married, and the other was a college freshman. They had gone around twenty minutes before.

Tommy's kid was nearly eight years old. My brother wasn't happy with the prospect of having a child so late in life, but he couldn't deny Emily anything she desired, and at the very least, he got his guy. Junior had been taken to the wedding ceremony but sent home with her parents before the reception.

"You got it right," my brother said, smiling. "Now, if you and your girlfriend would just quit cramping my style..."

"I'm not his girl," Jess said, snorting my brother.

"Fine," he answered, but Tommy being Tommy, he had to add, "Thanksgiving is this year at our place." I'm looking forward to one of your apple pies."

"After all these years, you'd think you'd remember that Jess's produces one of the greatest apple pies." Emily shook her head as she looked at her husband.

"Are you serious? I have nightmares about her apple pie."

"You know, it may imply something entirely different." Emily gave her husband a stern look. When he realized what she meant, his response was so Tommy.

"Please! I'll leave such dreams to my younger brother. You're nearly too much woman for me." Emily smiled, touched his face, and kissed him quickly. "Remember what I said about nearly."

"Have you changed at all, you two?" Jess's delight was palpable.

"Sure, we have," my brother said, but then turned to his wife and added, "Let's go!" Your parents will be joining us for breakfast with the kids tomorrow. We're destroying daylight!"

"Is it burning daylight?" Jess's perplexity was understandable. After all, it was completely dark.

"Quote from an old western. I'm shocked you missed it. He's implying that they just have a few hours to carry out his sinister intentions for Emily."

"Oh," Jess finally understood and smiled.

"I told my parents and the girls to come over for supper, not breakfast," Emily said to her husband with a beautiful grin. His joyful shout was amusing, but it didn't stop my sister-in-law from staring at me and saying, "Tommy's not the only one with sinister intentions for tonight."

"Sure, you two have switched loads," I muttered, turning her smile into a grin.

Tommy and Emily exchanged their goodbyes and immediately departed, which made sense given their intentions for one other. I was envious, but Jess was still sitting on the bench with my keys in her hand and wearing my jacket.

"You sat there." I didn't even bother to disguise my delight.

"I reasoned that I shouldn't drive. I'm not convinced I'm sufficiently sober." We both knew it was nonsense since dancing burnt up most of the alcohol in our systems, but I didn't say anything. Instead, I assisted her in getting up. Okay, so maybe I drew her in a little too close while doing it.

"If you kiss me again, I'll call a taxi." I found the fright in her eyes amusing. I laughed and took a step back.

"There'll be plenty of time for it later."

"We're not kissing anymore!" So, even though she was waiting for me, Jess was still processing what she was experiencing. Not so much for me. I'd never been so sure of anything in my life. Deep down, I knew she'd come to the same decision.

"Ever?" I couldn't help myself from taunting her, so I asked. I thought she would simply accept to spite me for a brief moment, but she quickly changed her mind.

"No, not tonight." I could tell she was serious by the tone of her voice. It was a condition she was attaching to her acceptance of a trip home. "And, given how effectively you handled the whole PDA issue, I want your word this time."

"It would most certainly not be a public exhibition of love," I smiled, emphasizing the term public. Jess shook her head and flushed. I believe she was amused, but it didn't make her back down from her demand. I gave myself a nod. "But don't worry, I'm not going to kiss you tonight. I will, however, take whatever kisses you are ready to provide."

"Keep dreaming," she taunted, a little more relaxed now that I'd promised. Jess was well aware that I was not the sort to break my promise. Of course, I was confident that not doing so would need a significant amount of work tonight.

"You've got no idea." For a long time, I'd been fantasizing about kissing Jess again. To be honest, I'd always felt a bit bad about it. I'd never cheated on Adrian, but I spent far too much time fantasizing about Jess when things became strained between us. Of course, I did not expect ever to see her again.

"I'm shivering. Let's get started." Jess gave the keys to me. When she changed the topic, I smiled and nodded. Allowing it was probably safer, but I didn't feel like playing it safe tonight. Still, I didn't say anything as I walked her to my vehicle. We were immediately in and out of the cold.

As my vehicle warmed up, Jess and I sat in quiet. We didn't know where to begin now that we were finally alone. There was a lot to say, but so much hinged on how the conversation went that I think both of us were afraid to move forward.

I exited the parking lot as soon as the windows cleared and the vehicle felt warm enough. I was staring at Jess nearly as much as I was at the road, but I was still hesitant to speak. That didn't stop me from reaching out and grabbing her hand. Fortunately, she didn't draw hers back. I grinned as I looked down at them.

"We haven't held hands in almost twenty-five years, yet it still seems natural." It was supposed to be a modest comment, maybe an ice breaker to ease us into our conversation. It did not go as planned.

"And who's to blame for that?" Jess's tone made it seem like a joke, but she wasn't laughing. When she was sad, she was always one to attempt to disguise her feelings. When we were younger, I was terrible at reading that about her. It was one of the reasons we used to quarrel so often, but I wasn't the naive child I used to be, and I realized what she was saying beneath her attempt at humor.

It startled me that she could be so outraged over something that occurred decades ago. I hated making her miserable, but I can't deny that it made me pleased since it showed she still cared.

"It's my mother's." Although I'm sure, Jess thought it wasn't simply an effort to lighten the atmosphere. She responded as one would anticipate.

"Don't even think of blaming your mum!" Jess attempted to pull her hand free this time, but I was prepared for it and refused to let go. "You cheated on me!"

"I didn't dump you," I said solemnly. "In reality, if I had ditched anybody at the time, it would have been Adrian. When we ran into one other, I was dating her. It was shortly after you graduated from college. I wanted to go on a date with you so strongly that I ended my relationship with Adrian, even though we had been dating for nearly a year and a half."

"There are two dates. That's all it took for you to decide to rush back to her." I despised the anguish I saw in Jess's eyes, but she had a right to feel, and I couldn't allow that to keep me from saying what needed to be said.

"I went on two dates, the second of which did not go well." It hadn't happened. I could still remember how disappointed I was afterward.

"And who was to blame for that?" Jess inquired once again, and this time I had no objection.

"It's mine," I acknowledged. "We attended Benny's party. You said you needed to go early since you had planned the following day, but I attempted to persuade you to remain when the time arrived. You declined."

"And that was our final conversation." Jess made a shaky motion with her head.

"I had to make the most difficult decision of my life. In hindsight, that was most likely the incorrect one, but..."

I didn't go too far before she cut me off. This conversion was not going as well as I had intended. When we were dancing, everything felt so beautiful. This was different and more difficult.

"Probably?" Jess chimed in; her irritation was palpable.

"It's all because of Bethany." It was the truth from God. I couldn't feel sorry for marrying Adrian since it gave me my daughter. It also shaped me into the guy I am now, for better or worse, but I wasn't going to say anything about it.

"All right," Jess responded more quietly. "I understand."

"But, just so you know, a lot of what occurred between us was my mother's fault," I couldn't help but add a wry smile. Jess shook her head this time.

"How do you calculate?"

"You and I have always had a tumultuous relationship," I stated. "We argued all the time, and let's just say I wasn't much fun to be around when that occurred. I was utterly heartbroken when I left for college, and we split up for the first time."

"And who was to blame?" she inquired a third time. That inquiry was beginning to irritate me.

"You ended our relationship." I knew it was wrong to say as soon as the words left my lips. I also knew what was causing it. It was the prospect of revisiting this experience. It was horrible enough when I repeated it in my brain, but now I'd have to do it in front of Jess.

"You were the one who went to college and slept with a harlot for the first week!"

"What else can I say? I was an eighteen-year-old idiot." "Frankly, some days, I fantasize of going back in time and kicking my foolish ass," I said, shaking my head. That made her grin, if only for a moment. I believe the fact that she could tell it was authentic helped her.

I probably should have stopped then, but I couldn't. If what we previously had was to be rekindled correctly, we needed to stop talking about it.

"We'd been arguing all summer, and this was my first trip away from home. College was frightening, and I'd been drinking a lot. For what it's worth, said'slut' came on to me, but we didn't go." Jess seemed to be about to say something, but I cut her off. "I do not deny that I cheated on you. I did, but I instantly regretted it. I informed you straight away, expecting that we could work things out, but instead, you dumped me."

"What did you anticipate? I felt wounded and enraged. It was my final year of high school, and I did not deserve for it to be devastated by my college boyfriend's infidelity!"

"No, you didn't," I said, swallowing and stopping to let her relax. "You had every right to be upset, but I was still madly in love with you. I was hoping that after you'd cooled down, you'd forgive me, and we'd be able to go on." I shook my head at the terrible recollection.

"I phoned you from college throughout the semester, before mobile phones. I had to use the hall phone, but nothing I said made any difference. You would not forgive me. It came dangerously close to destroying me."

"It wasn't a picnic, either," Jess answered. "And keep in mind that I was the one who was harmed."

"I understand," I said, blowing out a breath that was too forceful to be termed a sigh. "And, to be honest, I'm not making any excuses. I simply want you to understand what occurred from my perspective so you can appreciate why I made the choice I did." For a few seconds, we were both deafeningly quiet. Jess was the one who shattered it this time.

"You have yet to explain how your mother's responsibility is any of this." Her tone had softened. I'm sure she wasn't looking forward to revisiting that experience any more than I was. I also believe Jess was letting me know, in her way, that our breakup was a thing of the past and that she had forgiven me for my youth's folly.

I was very convinced Jess did that a few years after we split up. When we were home on break from college, we'd run into each other now and again. We even chatted for a long time once or twice, but we didn't get back together until after Jess graduated from college. Jess had her own life and pals at school, while I had mine.

"Well?" Jess suggested it. "What action did your mum take? This should go well."

It was a reasonable question, but answering it would require me to reveal something about myself to Jess that I wasn't very fond of. I'd thought about it more times than I could count, but it wasn't the same as confessing it aloud, particularly to Jess.

"It wasn't anything she did. It was what she didn't do that was the problem." Okay, my response was vague, but this was not a good time. "What are your thoughts on what transpired following that disastrous second date? The one where you had the stuff to do the following morning, and I attempted to get you to remain late despite having agreed to bring you home early."

"You phoned me once and left an ambiguous message. I returned your call, but you were not at home. I called you a few more times during the following several weeks, but you stopped responding to my calls. It felt as if you had vanished entirely. I discovered out you were engaged three months later."

That was very much what I expected to hear. I shook my head, ruminating on "what may have been." It took some effort to shrug off the gloomy thoughts and return to the topic of the talk.

"Adrian and I were together for a year and a half. By the time you and I ran into each other that final time, I'd already broken up with her twice, but she took me back each time. That's how much she adored me." I hated talking about it nearly as much as I despised cheating on Jess. "But it didn't stop me from breaking up with her for the third time that summer when I saw you. I was still hopelessly in love with you."

"So, why did you go back to her after that second date and propose to her?" It was a reasonable question, but it wasn't simple to respond to.

"I was ready to settle down," I said, gradually concluding my explanation. "I've always desired children and a family."

"And you weren't?"

"You were," I agreed, shaking my head at the thought. "It was self-evident."

"What occurred after that?" Jess was seated with her back against the vehicle door. At least, as much as her seat belt would allow. She seemed to be attempting to get as far away from me as possible, yet weirdly, she hadn't tried to tear her hand away from mine again.

"Being with you on those two occasions brought all of my anxieties back to the surface. Things I thought I'd outgrown in college." Her perplexed expression sought a more straightforward explanation. "Jess, you were always the most popular. I didn't hold it against you.

To be honest, I'm not sure why you decided to date me in the first place."

"As I recall, I invited you to the Sadie Hawkins dance." That remembrance brought a grin to my face. Back in the day, a Sadie Hawkins dance was a dance where the females got to invite the boys to attend. Today, I suppose they could do it whenever they wanted, but when I was younger, it was unusual.

"That's true, but we discussed my fears, not my luck." Jess didn't grin, but her eyes glowed a bit. It was past time to wrap things up.

"So there we were, dating again, both eager to settle down. The only thing was, you'd broken up with me five years before and refused to accept me back until after we graduated from college. I knew you wanted a family and children as much as I did. My issue was that I wasn't sure whether you still loved me."

"Pardon?"

"Jess, I was frightened you would settle for me," I eventually confessed. "And my ego couldn't handle it any longer. I didn't want that type of relationship as much as I loved you. To be honest, I didn't want to put myself through that type of pain." I became deafeningly quiet. What more could I possibly say?

"So you had to choose between Adrian, who loved you enough to forgive you for breaking up with her three times, and me, who you believed may settle for you."

"Exactly," I said, hoping that she had grasped what I was saying. She, unfortunately, did.

"You're a jerk!" Jess snapped, finally releasing her grip on her hand. But she went above and above. Jess did hit me in the arm. I was taken aback. It became much worse when she hauled off and did it again. It was everything I could do not to laugh at this point, but I knew it would be a tremendous mistake.

"Did anything so long ago justify two punches?" I was attempting to lighten the atmosphere. It was a colossal failure.

"Yes!" she yelled, clearly still enraged and contemplating beating me again, but mercifully she didn't. My shoulder ached, but I had earned it. I was relieved she stopped herself since I was scared she'd damaged her hand. "One for being too oblivious to how I felt about you."

"And what about the other?"

"The other," she said gently again. "That was your punishment for what you did to Adrian. She was never one of my favorite people, but she deserved better." That forced me to stop for a while.

"Yes, I did to her precisely what I was terrified you'd do to me. I made a decision." I shook my head before continuing, "You know, I truly liked her. I still do, but it's not the same as it was with you. I came up with a slew of excuses for it, but I knew the truth."

Jess slipped back into her seat, her rage gradually dissipating. I concluded that the best thing I could do was allow her time to process what I had told her. We sat in quiet, each of us immersed in our thoughts. I waited, but when she didn't say anything after about 10 minutes, I couldn't help but reach out and retake her hand. I was relieved when she agreed to allow me.

That's how we got the rest of the way to her place. Jess turned on music sometime in the middle. It allowed us to unwind, which I believe was something we both needed at the time.

After a little more than an hour, I stopped in front of Jess's house but didn't turn off the vehicle. I wasn't sure whether Jess would welcome me in, and I didn't want the night to end. I'm guessing she didn't since she didn't attempt to flee.

"You still haven't clarified what your mother was involved in all of this."

When I realized Jess was correct, I snorted. I hadn't told her why I had resented my mother for wrecking my life for so long. The funny aspect, or maybe the sad part, was that even though Mom had been gone for years and I loved and missed her every day, this was the one thing she did that still hurt me. I was never able to let it go.

"I was perplexed after our second date when Adrian and I started communicating again." I shook my head at the thought. "Whatever you want to say about her, Adrian was a rock in her own right, and her love was something I could count on, particularly when my anxieties showed. Add to that the fact that you never returned my call, and I was forced to make a choice."

Jess began to object, but I squeezed her hand to signal that I needed to finish what I said before discussing it.

"For some reason, I recall that information being the catalyst that drove me over the brink. I wasn't sure about your feelings for me, and you hadn't phoned. Adrian and I had split up, yet she was still there for me when I needed her. The option seemed easy at the moment, yet there was a part of me that refused."

"However, it is insufficient."

"No, not enough," I acknowledged reluctantly. "I used to tell myself that I'd chosen to marry the one who loved me unconditionally over the one settling for me. That's how I got through the rough patches with Adrian early on, and it seemed to work for the most part. It wasn't painless, but it worked."

"What has changed?" Jess was a wise lady.

"Adrian and I had been married about ten years when I went to see Mom and Dad by myself," I said, recalling how it felt as the floor collapsed under me. "I used to do it on weekends to get away from Adrian when we argued. I'm not sure how my parents and I got into the topic of my previous relationships, but when you came up, my mother casually confessed to not telling me you phoned a few times after our final date."

"Didn't she?" Jess inquired, evidently taken aback.

"Mom, it seems, recalled how heartbroken I was when you and I broke up in college and didn't want me to go through it again. She was also aware that Adrian and I were conversing once again." I waited patiently and saw Jess' countenance start to set in as I had said. It didn't take long for the anticipated eruption to occur.

"I still can't believe it. I loved your mum! How could she have?" Jess was in pain. That's what I thought. It was nothing compared to how I felt after learning the truth.

"I suppose Mom liked you in her way," I said before explaining. "But you and I argued all the time, and Adrian's love for me was evident to her. What could a mother desire more for her son?" We went silent for a few seconds while she processed what I said. I spent my time ruminating on the past and reliving the present. When Jess eventually broke the stillness, I was more than a little relieved.

"Your mother never told you I phoned, which made you question how I felt just enough to select Adrian," Jess replied, shaking her head in surprise. "You know, I believe you're correct. It is your mother's fault."

"Not really," I murmured, finally conceding the truth to her and myself. "Or, at the very least, just partly. I might have contacted you again, and things may have turned out differently if I had, but I was terrified of the same reason that made her not tell me." She was paying attention, but when I was through, Jess shook her head.

"No, that was unquestionably your mother's fault." I'm not sure why, but her tenacity made me giggle. That's when an unexpected notion occurred to me. I kept laughing, but it wasn't hilarious.

"Well, if we're going to blame her for my decision, we have to praise her for tonight."

"How do you calculate?" Jess inquired, apparently interested in what I was saying.

"It was terrible enough that Mom kept the fact that you phoned a secret, but then she revealed it to me years later. Do you realize what it did to me?" I could see the reality dawning on Jess, but I persisted in my explanation.

"When Adrian and I had our disagreements, I couldn't find tranquility after that. My grandiose rationale about choosing the lady who loved me unconditionally over someone who would have settled for me evaporated." I shook my head, frustrated at the amount of time squandered.

"You had taken the time to call me back. It didn't necessarily imply that we were destined to be together, but the concept lingered in the back of my mind. If that hadn't happened, I could still be married to Adrian."

"Not probable," Jess said. "You knew you weren't in love with her. Bethany was the only reason it lasted as long as it did." Jess seemed confident, and after some contemplation, I concluded she was probably correct. But I wasn't as sure as she was.

"It might have had something to do with the fact that you were already married to Robbie. It didn't matter whether I remained or went since you were gone to me."

"Robbie, don't bother reminding me!" Jess expressed her dissatisfaction with the situation with a shake of her head. "That was one of the worst decisions I've ever made. He was a kind person, but I only married him because I wanted children." We shared a glance, and I knew she told me I wasn't the only one who married for the wrong reasons.

"What transpired?" I inquired because I suspected she would need to discuss it. I'd spent a lot of time talking about Adrian.

"We put off having children for a few years to save for a home. Robbie was sure about it, and I couldn't dispute his reasoning, "Jess said, clearly remembering sad memories. I patiently waited for her to continue.

"And then, nothing, when it was time to try again." It pained to witness her grief, but all I could do was grip her hand and provide whatever consolation I could. "We were on our way to consult a reproductive specialist when it occurred. Christine and Robbie met." She took a hiatus and shook her head. "It was love at first sight, and our marriage was doomed."

"Please accept my apologies." They appeared to be the only words that suited. Her smile took me by surprise.

"It's alright," Jess said, breaking loose from the past. She clasped my hand again. "At the very least, it led to this moment."

"Life can indeed be strange, isn't it?" With a shake of my head, I inquired. She agreed with a nod.

"My main regret is that I never had children, but I made peace with it long ago."

"I wanted a lot more, but Adrian said no. She suffered from severe postpartum depression." I hesitated, recalling how difficult her unwillingness to have any more children was at the time.

One specific argument sprung into my head. It was the moment I realized Bethany would be an only child. It wasn't only that my ex-husband refused to have any more children. Adrian was terrified of going through another pregnancy and accompanying sadness. I found it out when she broke into tears and sobbed violently the last time we discussed it.

"You're fortunate to have Bethany." Jess's remarks jolted me back to the present.

"Yes," I said casually. There was no use in rehashing the 'what may have been' scenario. I'd been there too often to count, and it had never gone well. Growing up, I dreamed of having a large family and was confident that I would acquire one someday. Life, unfortunately, does not always go as planned. On the other hand, Bethany was a gift I never stopped admiring. "I am," I say.

It was time to attempt to lighten the atmosphere once again. "You know, we could always adopt if things between us work out." Jess shocked me once more. She responded far better than I had anticipated.

"I believe we're a bit old for that," she chuckled, adding, "Not that I won't hold you to that offer if it does work out between us by some miracle." I believe her statements stunned her more than me since she quickly added, almost ruefully, "So much for having made peace with not having any kids."

I was 51 years old, and Jess was 50. Part of me thought I was too old to create a family again, but it occurred to me that if Jess genuinely wanted to adopt, I'd do it. The bizarre thing was that, despite our age, I could imagine us establishing a family together.

Maybe it was simply my younger self's fantasies from when I first fell in love with Jess returning, or perhaps it was the prospect of sharing a kid with her, but what began as an effort at comedy was suddenly no longer humorous.

"You'd make an excellent mother." I believe the gravity of my remark jolted her back to reality.

"We were discussing how it would make sense for us to rekindle our relationship after all these years. We weren't referring to children. It's much too early for that discussion."

"Only if you say so."

"And we're much too old," Jess remarked hesitantly.

"Agreed." I also meant it, but she saw what I was saying. I noticed a brief flicker of familiarity as well as something else. I could feel when parts of her old dreams, presumably quite similar to mine, reawakened. It brought with it promise but also far too many bitter memories.

Jess understood deep down that if she genuinely wanted her children, I'd provide them to her in whatever way I could. The concept delighted her, but it also terrified her. When Jess opted to shift the topic, I understood.

"You explained why you remained with Adrian even though it was evident you didn't love her, but why didn't you contact me after your divorce?" It was an excellent question, but it wasn't readily answered, so I paused.

"When I learned about your divorce, I honestly considered leaving Adrian. I thought about it a lot, but there was Bethany and the fact that you and I hadn't communicated in about fifteen years at the time. I wasn't sure whether you'd be the same person or if you even remembered me."

Jess nodded in agreement, clearly deep in contemplation. "Is that why you didn't attempt to contact me after your divorce?" That was one of the reasons, but not the only one.

"We haven't seen each other in over twenty-five years. That's a long time. Sure, you loved me enough to call me back after our final date, which may have affected how things turned out, but that was long ago. I can't say I didn't fantasize about the prospect, but to attempt to find you? Do you realize how strange it would have been for me to walk up at your home unexpectedly?"

"Almost as insane as me attending your daughter's wedding." That effectively knocked the wind out of whatever rebuttal I might have provided.

"There is that," I confessed with a genuine chuckle, directed mainly at myself. "But, on the other hand, you've always been the bold one in our relationship."

"Not really," she said, her face suddenly gloomy. "When it came to us, I've always understood what I wanted." That stung. It was more painful than I wanted to confess. "Plus, to be honest, I don't believe I would have contacted you if Walt hadn't asked me to your daughter's wedding. It was too fantastic an opportunity to pass up. I told myself I was coming to check on you and your siblings. I pretended it was simply curiosity, but I knew it wasn't."

"I truly did consider contacting you," I remarked into the following hush. "But there was always an excuse to postpone it. Bethany's wedding provided a suitable justification. I didn't want to do anything that would add to the family's burden."

"At least, that's what I told myself, but I'm starting to suspect there's more to it." The following section would be challenging to get out, but so be it. "I was too smitten with the idea of us reuniting to face the risk of really doing so. I'd been clinging to you in my mind for so long that it had become a crutch that I couldn't let go of, and contacting you would have done just that. I believe I was too much of a coward to risk it in the end."

It was right there. Everything was there for her to see. I should have felt better by now, but I didn't. Tonight made me realize how much I wanted Jess back in my life, but it was all up to her now, and I'd done everything wrong up to this point. In college, I cheated on her. I didn't believe in her love after we graduated, and I was too afraid to pursue her when the time came. Oh my goodness! What an idiot I'd been.

"And now that you've seen me, what do you think?" I'd been lost in my recollections and self-analysis, looking out into space. I shoved the ideas away and returned my complete focus on Jess. I wanted her to understand what I was going through. It was time to quit acting like a fool and take a stand. Only, me being me, I began with humor.

"Do you mean you've found me down and let me know you still care?" My joking caused Jess to roll her eyes, which made me grin, but it didn't last long. Not because I wasn't joyful, but because the reality that Jess was back in my life was finally settling in, and I didn't want to squander it. My aspirations were on the verge of becoming a reality.

"Jess, being here with you is so much greater than even my dreams," I stated solemnly, looking at her to show how much I meant it. "I'm not leaving the house. I adore you." There. It was something I'd said. I knew it was ridiculous, but the truth was the truth, and I was done messing up with Jess by keeping my sentiments to myself. "I've never stopped falling in love with you."

"Do you realize how insane that sounds?" My heartbeat quickened as I realized I'd done it again and lost my chances with Jess, but this was too essential for anything less than the truth.

"Of course," I said with a shrug, thinking she'd get it. Jess gradually smiled, and I realized she did. My heart rate increased once again.

"All right," she replied gently. "Because I believe I, too, am insane. I don't want to be the only one." She stretched out and laid her free hand on mine, still clutching her other hand. "You see, I still adore you."

I urgently wanted to kiss Jess right then and there, but I'd promised not to. I took a look at my watch. The time was 11:45 a.m. Jess frowned briefly as a result of the action.

"Don't even think about it because tonight doesn't end at midnight! It concludes at daybreak." It should have astonished me how easily Jess picked out what I was thinking, but it didn't. She could always tell what I was thinking.

"I can wait," I responded but added firmly, "Out here in the vehicle if necessary."

"You're not going to be sitting in your vehicle all night!" Jess's eyes glowed with delight. She didn't seem to believe me. "And you're not going in."

"I want a kiss, and as I already said, I'm not going away." This time, she saw the reality and trusted me.

"There's so much we need to catch up on," Jess replied, attempting to shift the conversation.

"Do you truly believe any of it will affect how we feel?" Jess replied even though it was a short, rhetorical inquiry.

"No," she acknowledged softly, her warm smile spreading to and through me. Jess had also finally moved her gaze away from the automobile door. "We haven't seen each other in twenty-five years, but that hasn't changed our feelings for one other. I don't see our saying anything about what occurred to us at that period accomplishing anything, either." Jess was getting near. I was dying for a kiss, but I wouldn't violate my promise. It was critical not to squander this opportunity.

Jess leaned in closer and smirked as she realized what she was doing to me. Her lips were just a few inches from mine, and her eyes shone in a manner that I recall well.

"You should realize that I am merely human."

Jess's grin deepened in response to my remark, but she didn't laugh or drawback. Instead, she drew her chin up and mashed her lips on mine. I was so taken aback that it took me a second to reciprocate her kiss, but something deep within me sparked once I did. Jess and I had kissed earlier, but it was more out of passion than anything else. This was all about love, love, and dedication. That didn't stop the urge from reappearing with vigor a few seconds later.

We stayed in one other's arms and kissed for so long that my lips hurt when we eventually parted. Jess was the one who took a step back. I would have remained like that all night if I had the opportunity.

"You said you'd take whatever kisses I offered." Jess's remarks made me gently chuckle.

"Yes, I did," I readily replied. "But I didn't expect us to behave like adolescents by steaming up the vehicle windows."

"Does it constitute a complaint?" Jess inquired, her brow furrowed.

"Difficultly," I sneered. "Teens have been known to do more than simply kiss in a vehicle if memory serves."

"Forget it!" she said. "We're both too old for anything like that!"

"Not tonight," I stated more seriously than I had intended. "Tonight, I feel young again, and it's all because to you." I grabbed for Jess, but she shocked me by springing out of the vehicle and flinging open the door on her side. As she raced toward her residence, she slammed the door and giggled. I jumped out of the car and ran towards her. It was a natural response.

I just returned to myself when I approached her. I halted when Jess opened her front door, concerned that I'd made a mistake. I'd told myself that I wouldn't push her tonight. Was she going to hold me accountable for that?

Jess entered, leaving the door open. She returned with a promise-filled grin moments before she vanished, confirming the implicit invitation. She must have changed her mind about allowing me in.

I followed Jess inside the room and closed the door behind me. Her eyes twinkled mischievously as she waited for me just out of sight.

"Are you sure?" I asked myself.

"I believe we're both at an age to know what we want." She was solemn, but I couldn't help but smile with relief.

"So, are you saying you're not going to hold me to my word? Can I kiss you right now?"

"Please," Jess said, her breath stopping in her throat as she raised her head forward, offering her lips to me. I lowered my head and mashed my lips against hers. The burning heat between us erupted into something considerably more fierce. As she placed her arms around my neck, I moaned.

I wasn't a young guy anymore, yet there were moments when I forgot. This was one of those occasions. I stretched out and took Jess in my arms. She whimpered but never broke our kiss. I dragged her down the corridor, supposing her bedroom was in that direction.

The first room we came to was not it. Jess merely interrupted our kiss to whisper, "The last one on the right."

We had some trouble getting there since neither wanted to stop kissing. I almost clipped her head in the doorway as we entered her room. Jess was aware but didn't appear to care. I expected her to taunt me about it afterward, but that was an issue for another time. I'm carrying her to her bed and laying her down. Jess's eyes were greedy as she stared up at me. It was something I'd never forget seeing.

I joined her, and our kisses became more intense as we struggled to pull each other out of our clothing. It would have been amusing if our need hadn't been so dire. What was I thinking? It was funny in any case. I didn't know how long it had been for Jess, but it had been much longer than I cared to accept.

It didn't take long for Jess's bare body underneath mine. I stopped kissing her long enough to look her in the eyes. To be honest, I couldn't stop myself.

"I'm not as youthful as I used to be," she said, a bit self-consciously, unusual.

"Please!" I laughed and snorted. "You have a physique that most twenty-year-olds would want." Jess was always the sort to look after herself, and she looked fantastic. Understand me. It's not that age hadn't taken its toll, but the changes in her physique simply added to my fascination. "My God, you are so lovely!"

"You adore me." It was an effort at a joke, but it didn't go well with me.

"Yes, I do," I said solemnly. "However, the truth is the truth. I will spend the rest of my life demonstrating to you that you are the most gorgeous lady I've ever known."

"That seems interesting."

As our lips met again, I leaned down on Jess, enveloping her body with mine. I loved the sensation of her under me. Jess exposed herself to me, and I wanted to explore everything she had to offer, but I couldn't take my lips away from hers. Her scent was just too enticing.

I'm not sure how long we lay there fervently kissing, my chest crushed against her large breasts, my erection rubbing against her mound without really entering her. When Jess wrapped her legs around me and attempted to pull me into her, I knew she was desperate.

I knew I wouldn't last long once I entered Jess, so I began kissing my way down her body instead of succumbing. When I got to her breasts, I grinned. Jess gasped as I gently squeezed one of her nipples and fastened my teeth on the other. They were usually sensitive, and I'd forgotten how much she enjoyed what I was doing.

"It's not fair!" Jess sobbed. I moved my free hand between her thighs and teased the top of her entrance until I was sure her first orgasm of the night was ready to burst out. I sucked on her nipple briefly before biting down even harder and sliding my hand over her nub, two fingers thrusting inside of her. "Oh. Oh my goodness!"

I can't describe how fantastic it felt to see Jess's body tensing and exploding in relief. I hadn't made a lady lose control and come that hard in a long time. It was such a heady sensation that I decided to repeat it before achieving my release. I felt sure that I could. It had been over thirty years since we had made love, but Jess was my first, and all of her likes and dislikes were imprinted on my mind. Furthermore, her body was responding much more strongly than I recalled.

Once she'd recovered enough to appreciate what I was doing, I kissed my way down from her breasts. Jess exclaimed when my lips and tongue stroked her lower tummy, but she attempted to stop me.

"You can't!" she exclaimed. "I wasn't expecting it, and it's been a long time." I was perplexed by the unexpected mixed-signal and paused until she continued, "I haven't shaven in a long time." Did she genuinely believe that was important to me?

"You say it as if it's a terrible thing," I teased, nuzzling closer. I know a lot of ladies these days remove the hair between their legs, but I was old school. I felt the hair there to be appealing and ladylike.

"But..." I disregarded Jess because the resistance in her legs went away, and she let me open them despite what she said. She was interested in what I was going to do.

Jess had a tiny, black bush between her legs, but it wasn't very dense. I had no clue why she had responded the way she did until I saw a few grays mixed in. Was she expecting that to affect me? Just though being with her made me feel youthful didn't mean I was blind to the years that had gone by since our previous encounter.

My passion for her was heightened because she had a few gray hairs. They reminded me of the time we'd squandered away and how happy we were to be back together, but they were also curiously attractive. Jess, on the other hand, captivated me in every way. We were older and maybe wiser was why I was finally sure we were destined to be together.

"Mine!" I hissed, forcing my tongue into her black patch and stroking it up and down the whole length of her gap. Jess gasped loudly, her legs stretched even wider apart. She was already wet, but she rapidly got saturated as I worked hard to bring her to her second climax. Her flavor appealed to me!

Jess's perfume was so strong that I lost count of time as I inhaled deeply. I could have remained like that forever, but Jess reached for my head with both hands. Her fingers were intertwined in my hair, and she yanked my lips firmly on her mound. I pushed my tongue deep into her mouth, feeling her opening twitch as her fluids spewed out.

"Yes!" Jess sobbed as her whole body clenched and shuddered. That didn't stop me from going on. When Jess cried out again a few seconds later, I was pleasantly pleased.

"Not this time!" Her body erupted into another orgasm as she thrashed under me so violently that she tangled her blankets. This climax was considerably drier than the last one. I drank as much as I could, but I wore quite a bit.

Jess drew me up once she had regained control. She wiped her tears from my cheeks with one hand before pressing her lips to mine. She couldn't possibly have gotten it all, but I believe her need for a kiss was too powerful to resist. My yearning was so intense that I pushed her lips open and inserted my tongue hungrily inside.

Jess was tired, but it didn't stop her from reciprocating my passionate kiss. She ultimately grabbed my hardness in her fingers and stroked it.

"I'm not going to be around for long," I cautioned. My need for release was on the verge of taking control. I hadn't forgotten how enjoyable it was to be with Jess, but I hadn't anticipated it to improve so much over time. Her mere presence was driving me insane.

"Good!" Jess gave me a passionate grin and moved down my body. We'd learned about sex together, and by the time we split up, she'd acquired a skilled tongue. I wasn't let down as she curled her lips over my length. But I don't recall Jess doing it while gazing up at me. No woman had done so. Usually, all I could see was the back of someone's head. This was much superior!

"Wow, that's very hot!" I sighed as I watched Jess gently bob her head up and down. The scene had me completely captivated.

"I thought you said you weren't going to last long?" she teased, temporarily releasing her lips.

"No, I'm not!" I exclaimed, reaching out and yanking her back down on me. Jess sexily grinned and took my entire length into her throat. Her lustful black eyes never left mine.

That was the limit of my tolerance. Without warning, I lost control. As my climax kicked in, my hips rose off her bed. Jess's grin grew greedy as she swallowed the first few spurts of my release. It was allowed to her that there was more than that. I hadn't gone this far in years.

Jess yanked off my cock and stroked it while I covered her breasts. She was smiling with a lustful and satisfied expression that was uniquely hers. I was almost finished when she brought my hardness back to her lips, but she didn't take it in this time.

Instead, her tongue snaked out, and she rubbed it over my cock's head, drawing out the rest of my climax. Another lengthy stream of cum erupted, surprising Jess and striking her on the face. Despite the severity of the situation, she arched an eyebrow and gave me a look that made me giggle. That didn't stop her from cleaning her face with her sticky fingers and reaching for her lips. It would have exploded if I had anything left in me, but I was drained.

I watched as Jess wiped the come from her chest with the linen. I enjoyed how the weight of her breasts drew them down just a little. I concentrated on them until Jess used her tongue to wipe the remainder of my sperm off my cock. I had forgotten about her chest and pretty much everything else. I assumed she was doing it, but I realized she wasn't when she didn't stop after a few seconds. Jess had determined that we weren't quite finished.

I wasn't a spring chicken, and I would have been concerned about my ability to react to her evident desire if it had been anybody else, but it wasn't. It was Jess, and she was staring up at me with smoldering eyes once again. Nonetheless, I was shocked at how rapidly I healed and got tough again. So much for being exhausted.

"Excellent!" Jess smiled as she let go of my rigidity in her lips. She then shifted position on the bed, straddling my hips. Her gaze was fixed on mine as she rocked back and forth, squeezing the length of my cock between her legs but not yet allowing me within.

I sat back comfortably with my hands behind my head while I watched her tease me. Her body didn't take long to start reacting. As her juices began to flow again, she glided more effortlessly over my length.

Jess reached down and moved my cock to her entrance, her gaze never leaving mine. The love of my life slipped down my whole length till most of her black thatch of hair between her knees brushed on me.

"Wow!" she exclaimed. "I don't recall ever feeling that full."

"Flattery will get you anywhere," I mused, half-laughing, half-groaning. Jess grinned and shook her head before rising and sitting back down. When I was totally inside of her again, she groaned. She repeated the move a few more times, becoming more at ease with it.

"A girl may become used to this."

"I hope so!" I moaned as I transferred my hands to her hips and assisted Jess as she rode me gently.

She eventually slumped forward and stopped herself by putting her palms on my chest. Her lips parted as she accelerated her ride on me. As she bounced up and down my length, her breathing got more ragged. I couldn't have lasted as long as I did if Jess hadn't previously taken care of me, but I knew I wouldn't survive much longer.

"Jess, I'm almost there!"

"Good!" she said, a passionate grin on her face. "I want to feel you into me!"

I yanked her down, pressing my lips against hers. As I flipped us over to be on top of her, Jess groaned into my lips. I might have questioned whether she was confident, but the fire in her eyes answered my silent query. It was evident to her that I wanted the same thing. I tried to fill her, to own her for me now and forever. I made a deep push.

Jess yelled out, but that didn't stop me from pulling out and repeating the process. When I felt her nails scrape my back, I grinned with delight. She always did it when she was about to have a massive orgasm.

"It feels so nice!" she said to wrap her legs around my hips. I drew out and plunged deep, again and again, pushing us both to the verge but holding back for as long as possible.

Jess scraped my back once again with her nails. I seized her hands this time and pressed them on the bed, above her head. Jess gasped loudly and pressed her lips against mine. I reciprocated her lustful kiss for a few seconds, but we couldn't go on with me pushing in and out of her so furiously. Jess lowered her head to the bed.

"Finish me!" she cried out. "Please!"

We couldn't kiss as we worked, but we could look at each other as our expected release date approached. Jess was panting and swaying her head from side to side. As I drove deep, again and over, my breathing became more strained.

"Come on in!" Jess inquired. "I want to feel like you're filling me up."

"You're all mine!" I roared, claiming Jess with all my might like I should have done years ago.

"Yes!" she exclaimed. "Yours, forever and ever!"

I let go of Jess's hands and plummeted once more. She began to tremble under me as I lost it, filling her with all I had left. My cum boiled without a hitch. Jess's body spasmed under me in acceptance. Our bodies thrashed against one other until we were exhausted.

Jess's legs were still wrapped around my hips when we were finished. She'd been using them to drag me as far as possible. As we finished, I bent down and placed my lips to hers. She wrapped her arms over my neck and shoulders. We kissed tenderly as the intensity faded, yet it never totally vanished with Jess.

"I'd forgotten how amazing it could feel," I said as I rolled off her and onto my back.

"Me as well." Jess moved closer to me and rested her head on my shoulder. She also drew the cover-up, leaving the sheet at the foot of the bed. It was in no condition to be helpful.

"That was wonderful," I remarked, feeling utterly exhausted in a friendly manner for the first time in a long time. "You are amazing!"

"You're not too awful yourself," groggily responded Jess. I leaned forward and kissed the top of her head.

"I adore you, Jessica." As a result, she nuzzled deep into my shoulder and chest.

"You'd better," she warned, and despite my tiredness, I smiled. "Now go to bed."

I was fatigued and drained to an extent I had never imagined, yet I didn't fall asleep. Jess's head lying on my shoulder felt too wonderful. I laid there for at least twenty minutes, loving the actuality of the situation much more than any daydream I used to have about her.

"Are you unable to sleep?" Jess's question caught me off guard. I assumed she'd already passed out. Perhaps she's taken a power sleep. She did sound sleepy.

"Not yet," I said, bending in and kissing her cheek.

"Are you concerned? You are not required to be." As she raised her head and gazed into my eyes, I had no clue what she was talking about. "I'm sorry, I shouldn't have forced you to come within me, but I needed to feel genuinely desired. It's been a long time." I attempted to speak, but she covered my lips with her fingers as her face became sorrowful. "Robbie and I tried for children for a year when I was much younger. I can't become pregnant, and even if I could, I wouldn't force you..." I drew my fingers away from my lips.

"Jess, what part of my saying I love you and would never leave you again did you miss?" I inquired, irritated and a bit wounded.

"It's true, but I shouldn't have..."

With a kiss, I hushed her. She returned it fast enough, but I could sense she was still hesitant. I refused to accept it, so I rolled over her again.

"What are you up to?" She groaned again as I moved the head of my cock up and down her middle. I was cautious since I assumed she was a bit sore at this point, but that didn't stop her body from responding. "I couldn't do that again! I'm utterly exhausted." Despite her words, her legs extended to me.

I kissed Jess passionately and continued to do so until her body reacted as I expected. I gradually worked my way inside of her. We moved more gently this time, loving the sensation of our bodies crushed against one other. As we drove in unison, our lips stayed locked together. Our desire grew with time, but neither of us accelerated the pace. Still, there was only so long I could go without being released from what we were doing.

"Jess, I'm almost there again." It was the first time our lips had split since I slid back on top of her. Hers seemed to be swollen and chapped. I'm sure mine wasn't much better.

"Me too!" she said, our gazes locked.

"I'm going to come back within you." I wanted her to know that it was my decision this time, that I intended to give her what she desired, if at all possible. To express how much she meant to me. "I've always wanted more children and to have them with you..."

"I told you I couldn't have babies!" she said as I moved in and out of her warm embrace.

"You're not sure whether that's true." Jess is a wuss. She wanted what I was providing, but she was also terrified, fearful of how I'd respond if she became pregnant, and afraid of how I'd react if she didn't.

"But what if it is?" she questioned, her gaze fixed on me.

"If that's what you want, we'll adopt." I waited to make sure she understood what I was saying. "Jess, you're the love of my life, and I'll do anything for you as long as it's within my ability. That is something you must believe." Her expression softened.

A wise man would have stopped then, but who said I was smart? "But I'm still not certain you can't have children, so let's imagine 'boy.' A son would be fantastic!"

"I'm too old to have a kid!" says the mother. She groaned, but she wrapped her legs around me again, drawing me close. "After all, I've always desired a female!"

"Boy!" I persisted, eventually accelerating my speed.

"Girl!" she replied, her nail raking down my back.

Jess and I were always the sort of relationship that would debate, sometimes fiercely. That seemed unlikely to alter very soon. Then then, so much else had changed that it didn't matter.

"I adore you, Jessica!" When my release was just a few seconds away, I moaned.

"Love. You, as well!" Jess screamed as her orgasm erupted. My body followed, and we thrashed together until we were both exhausted. This time, Jess had to assist me in rolling off of her.

"You're going to kill me," I grumbled, feeling truly satisfied for the first time in ages.

"You?" she wailed. "You see, I'm not as youthful as I used to be."

"No one is ever." I chuckled softly. "But you're even more lovely than I remember, and the prospect of spending the next few decades with you gives my life a whole new purpose."

"How about a few of decades?" she sneered. "Make it a few, particularly if I become pregnant by some miracle. We don't want our children to lose their parents while they are young."

"Yes, my sweetheart." I laughed, but Jess didn't get it.

"Which means you need to start taking better care of yourself," she said. "You're in terrific condition for a guy your age, but I saw all the red meat you ate at the wedding for supper. You'll have to reduce your consumption."

"Never in a million years," I answered, reclining on my back and pushing her head back onto my shoulder, my arm about her. I enjoyed the sensation of her body against mine.

"We'll have to see." I couldn't help but grin because that was so Jess. It didn't hurt that she cuddled into my shoulder, even more when she said it. I was in such a good mood that I gave Jess the last say. There would be plenty of time afterward to continue the debate.

We lay there for a few minutes, feeling her gently fading away. I knew it wouldn't be long until I joined her, but I was too engrossed in the moment to fight sleep, even if just a little. Later, I kissed the back of Jess's head just as I felt myself drifting away.

"Jess, you have no clue how much having you back in my life means to me." The words came out of nowhere. They were the most sincere words I'd ever said. I was taken aback when she genuinely reacted.

"You?" Jess said sluggishly. "I knew I'd been waiting for this moment for nearly twenty-five years as soon as I saw you at the wedding. All that squandered time..."

I understood exactly what she meant. I couldn't begrudge the life I had, but it didn't mean I didn't miss out on all the time I could have spent with her.

"I promise," I murmured gently, my heart pounding. "No more squandered time." Jess exhaled softly and fell asleep again.

*****

"Neil, the Dad, reports that the steaks are about done, and everything else is ready. Jessica, how far out are you?" Despite her worried countenance, Bethany shone in the way that pregnant women frequently do.

It was a lovely summer day. My daughter was four months pregnant with her first kid, and my family and I were enjoying a cookout. What more could a guy want?

Bethany was finally beginning to emerge. It never stopped astounding me that my tiny daughter had her kid. I also wanted to argue that she was still too young, but Bethany and Neil had been married for over four years before choosing to raise a kid.

"Dad?" When I didn't respond, Bethany inquired. I suppose I'd been immersed in contemplation for a more extended period than I realized.

"She should've arrived 10 minutes ago." I wasn't very concerned. Jess was always late for everything. It took some getting accustomed to, but she was well worth the effort.

"Mom is at the corner light." Maisie was speaking while gazing down at her phone. My soon-to-be adopted daughter was nearly eleven years old and already stunning. She was playing Kan Jam in the yard with her cousin Tommy Junior.

"Thank you, little sis," Bethany said, sighing. I grinned at both of my girls. I was relieved to see how well they got along.

About three months after we reconnected, Jess and I married at a justice of the peace. There didn't appear to be any need to wait and plenty of reasons not to. We were no longer spring chickens, and Jess was the love of my life. That became clearer with each passing day. Besides, none of us wanted a large ceremony. It was their dedication to one another that was important.

A few years later, we looked into the adoption procedure. Jess yearned for a child of her own. As it turned out, there were a lot of regulations and limits to follow, particularly for a couple of our age. Most of them might be avoided by taking an older kid, but even this may take years and a lot of money. On the other side, being foster parents only took us four months.

Jess was first hesitant, but it didn't take much convincing her since she still wanted a daughter, and having one at that time was obviously out of the question. Sunny, our point of contact with the foster care system, was an accommodating lady who understood our desires to foster-to-adopt. The instant Jess lay eyes on Maisie, I knew everything would be OK. For both of them, it was love at first sight.

Unfortunately, it took Maisie six months to accept it. It was a problematic half-year, but things calmed down after that. I'm sure Jess's unwavering affection for the child helped.

Maisie was a simple kid to adore. She had emotional troubles due to all she'd gone through, but don't we all?

The legal concerns surrounding her release so that she could formally become a member of our family were eventually settled a few months ago. The official adoption was supposed to be completed by the summer, but she'd been our daughter from the minute we lay eyes on her.

"She's adorably cute."

I turned and smiled at my ex, seated with Don at the picnic table. According to Bethany, they hadn't married yet, but it was only a question of semantics. I was delighted for them.

"Thank you," I said with a grin. Adrian, being Adrian, couldn't stop there.

"I still think you're insane for starting over, but each to their own."

I nodded in agreement. Adrian and I had never been true friends, but it was conceivable now that we were divorced and had both moved on. Worse things had occurred. It was also clear why we didn't work. We didn't have the same goals in life.

Many people thought Jess and I were insane for starting over in our fifties, but it worked for us, and we were both old enough not to care what others thought.

"Here." As he sat in the lawn chair next to me, my brother offered me a fresh beer. "Neil is just getting ready to leave the BBQ."

"Good," his wife Emily remarked, her gaze fixed on his drink as she set the salad on the table. "You may benefit from some food in you." My sister, Mary, who was following her with one of the side dishes, smiled but didn't say anything. She's a wise lady.

Tommy rolled his eyes as he stared at me. I tried hard not to chuckle. It was never a good idea to get on Emily's wrong side, and she wasn't entirely incorrect. Tommy wasn't yet drunk, but he was well on his way.

"Where has your better half gone?" I questioned my sister, knowing that changing the topic was the best option.

"Bob will not arrive until after supper. He needed to get to the workplace."

"That guy doesn't understand the notion of weekends," my brother grumbled. Bob had his own business and worked hard hours regularly, but he always made time for Mary. He was helpful to my sister. I liked him, which was fortunate since Jessica had introduced them. My wife was already talking about wedding bells for them, but only time will tell.

"Mom is here," Maisie said, returning her gaze to her phone. "She says she needs some assistance carrying in the desserts." She quickly began going toward the gate. Tommy nearly jumped from the lawn chair and raced past my daughter.

"Please notify her that we are on our way!" My brother had an insatiable sweet taste, particularly when he was drunk.

"Don't eat anything on the way in!" Emily yelled after him, but I suspected she was wasting her time.

"I'll pitch in as well." Tommy Junior swiftly followed in the footsteps of his father and cousin. He wasn't a dummy. My brother would accept anything Jess gave him.

I took a little longer to get out of my lounge chair. Because, in part, I'd had my fair share of drinks, but mainly because I didn't want to destroy my appetite with dessert. I was looking forward to the steaks Neil was about to finish. It wasn't that I didn't eat red meat anymore, but it wasn't very frequently with Jess.

"He's simply a huge child," he says. Sarah, my niece, sighed as she put a bowl of food on the table. I was trying hard not to chuckle. Tommy's youngest daughter resembled her mother. His oldest daughter was more like him, but she couldn't come today. It was her husband's father-in-birthday. law's

"He's always been," Màry remarked with a smile. "It's one of his few redeeming characteristics." My sister-in-law said something that was most likely harsh based on her facial expression, but I was out of hearing at the time.

They were all on their way back when I arrived at the gate, so I suppose I was going slower than I anticipated. Tommy and Junior were holding tinfoil-wrapped dishes, but they were also nibbling on what I assumed were stolen oatmeal chocolate chip cookies. Their second favorite of Jess's sweets was directly behind her apple pie.

I smiled when I saw my wife behind them holding the apple pie, most likely to safeguard it from the 'Viking Horde.' When Tommy and Junior were in this mood, Emily nicknamed them that.

Jess's presence always made me joyful. She saw my gaze and grinned before pausing to deliver me the apple pie, but not before a brief kiss. The contact of her lips on mine still gave me a rush.

"You're running late." Jess didn't answer, so I suppose she regarded my statement as more of an observation than an accusation. Either that, or she felt a change of topic would be a better option.

"Maisie, did you use lotion? You've seen how rapidly she burns." Despite her dark hair and eyes, our baby had a lighter complexion than us. Her skin was very sun sensitive.

"Yes," I said with a grin and a head shake. "Twice. Emily did it at least once more shortly after we arrived, and I believe Mary slipped Maisie into the house and did it again about a half-hour ago. With all of the lotion she's applying, she appears pasty." When my wife discovered I'd be taking Maisie to the party by myself, I'm sure she called both of her sisters-in-law.

"Better to be cautious than sorry. We cannot let her burn again."

"You know, you'll have to forgive yourself for it at some point?" Masie suffered a nasty sunburn shortly after joining us. Jess was upset with herself. That's what I thought. I blamed myself as well. The only difference was that I forgave myself. "I've learned my lesson. Allow it to leave."

"I know, I know, but I still see her..."

"Isn't it fun to be a parent?" I made a sly interjection, which made her grin. "Just sit tight! Masie is just a few years away from being an adolescent. The real fun starts at that point."

"Please don't remind me." Jess giggled nervously as I drew her in for a second kiss with my free hand. We both glanced toward our daughter, who was lagging the rest of the group since she was holding Jake's hand and guiding him to the yard. Our three-year-old son loved his sister Masie.

I was somewhat aback by how successfully she adapted to the position of bigger sister. Masie was great with Jake, even when she wasn't sure about us for the first six months. The fact that he was our biological son didn't seem to upset her. I hoped it was because she recognized we couldn't love her even if she had the same DNA as us, but only time would tell.

"Are you going to tell me what you were doing this morning?" As the youngsters passed us, I asked Jess. It was more for my amusement than anything else. I wanted to grab both youngsters and embrace and kiss them, but they were too adorable. Since I hadn't seen Jake since earlier that morning, I leaned down and planted a brief kiss on top of his head as he passed.

"I went to the doctor with Jake for a checkup." Jess was tenderly beaming down at our children, which I appreciated, but I knew part of it was because she didn't want to look at me.

"You had the day's first appointment. That suggests you came to a halt someplace else after that." I had a feeling something was up with Jess. It wasn't all that horrible. She would have informed me if it was true, but she was concealing something from me, which was unusual.

"Later," she said, picking up the pace. "Masie texted that the dinner was nearly ready to be served. I didn't want to irritate Bethany." Jess and my elder daughter had an odd connection. They generally got along well, but today Adrian was present, so it was a bit more strained. Jess and Adrian were always courteous to one other, but they'd never be friends.

I felt horrible for Bethany since having all of us around was difficult for her, but she was the one who invited us all. I suppose she hoped things would grow better with time. Stranger things had occurred.

As she passed the kids, Jess grabbed Jake and started carrying him. Masie had the same treatment. My younger daughter rolled her eyes and then began to chuckle. It may have been because I was tickling her.

Masie had taken a while to trust me enough to let me do anything like that, and it may not last long since she was growing older so quickly, but I was going to savor as many moments like it as I could squeeze into her life. Masie had every right to chuckle.

We joined the others on the terrace, putting the kids down. Jess said hi, and I was about to return to my beach chair when my son-in-law walked over from the BBQ with a big tray of steaks.

"Okay, everyone. It's finally time to eat! Take a seat." Neil smiled as he positioned the steaks in the middle of the table.

"You must be in Heaven," Jess exclaimed as we sat down, knowing how much I appreciated a nice steak despite her best efforts to keep red meat out of my diet.

"You have no idea," I answered, but my gaze was fixed on her rather than the steaks. Jess grinned and, for a little while, flushed. She understood what I meant.

"No personal digital assistants!" Tommy interrupted when he saw how we were gazing at each other, which was absurd given that Jake was seated between us. He was no longer in a high chair. I missed it some days because, like most three-year-olds, he refused to sit still. Masie sat at the table with her cousins.

Still, my brother's mocking reminded me of the night Jess, and I bonded at Bethany and Neil's wedding. I'm sure that was also the night Jess, and I became pregnant with Jake, so we married a few months later. We may have hurried the wedding by being married at a justice of the peace and not having a large reception, but Jess did not want to seem pregnant in our wedding photographs.

After Jake was delivered, the doctor informed Jess and me that the "store was closed." Our kid was born healthy, but it had taken a toll on Jess, and he didn't want us to try again. Despite her age, Jess was disappointed, but I refused to consider going against the doctor's directions. I couldn't bear the thought of losing Jess. When I learned she genuinely did want more children, I suggested we look into adoption.

I was sitting back after dinner, enjoying the aftereffects of a nice steak and watching my family interact. Adrian seems to be having a good time as well. She didn't have any siblings, and I believe she missed mine.

It was incredible that she was here, mainly because I could see how pleased my older daughter was. Bethany was sitting at the other end of the table, doing the same thing I was. Our gazes locked, and we exchanged a father-daughter grin that lasted until Neil's large head came in the way. He finished his meal and snatched a brief kiss from his pregnant wife.

I looked over to my wife, who was using a wipe to clean Jake's hands now that he had finished creating a mess... I mean eating. As I observed the two of them, I smiled contentedly.

"I like Aisha, Momma. What happened to her?" It was such a simple question. During a gap in the discourse at the table, my kid said it. Jess's expression of surprise was priceless.

"Aisha?" Masie inquired, her eyes wide with curiosity. "Aisha was the name of my foster sister at the time." Jess didn't moan, but she wanted to.

"I understand." My wife was staring at me with trepidation, which was unusual for Jess. "She's meant to be going on to another foster family; it turns out. Sunny contacted us to enquire whether we wanted to adopt another kid. Aisha's paperwork was already completed, but I told her no since we felt that two children were more than enough." The reality gradually dawned on me.

"Would you have been there after Jake's doctor checkup this morning?" It was a question, but I'd wager a lot that I already knew the answer.

"Sunny has been so kind to us that I couldn't possibly refuse her meeting invitation." Everyone was looking at us, but I ignored them and concentrated on my wife.

"And the reason you didn't tell me was..."

"There was no need for me to disturb you. I was just meeting Sunny to be polite. What was the purpose if we promised not to adopt any more children?"

I genuinely felt myself thinking in my thoughts, 'Wait for it... Wait for it...' I didn't get beyond the third reiteration.

"Sunny, on the other hand, brought Aisha with her, and the young child is adorable. She's seven years old and hasn't had an easy existence."

"Her mother died when she was a baby," Masie said, seeming older than her years. "And her father was a jerk. She has burn scars down her side." If at all possible, the packed table got quieter.

Bethany's eyes welled up with tears. Mary seemed irritated, which was typical of my sister. Tommy had a solemn expression, which was unusual for him. Everyone else fits into one of those groups to some extent.

"She's been acting out lately," Jess said into the ensuing silence. "Sunny believes it started when Masie departed."

"Aisha needs someone to look after her." My younger daughter's face of despair was terrible.

"Someone she trusts, like you," Jess continued, proudly looking at Masie. The young woman reddened slightly and shrugged.

"I remember when I was a youngster, and the older kids were cruel," Masie said. "That was not fair to me. As I grew older, neither did the littles, so I became their buddy. The small ones are constantly in need of one."

I finally realized where Masie learned to be such a wonderful big sister. Every day, she amazes me more and more. I was optimistic that if I had been reared in her circumstances, I would not have turned out half as well as my youngest daughter. Sure, she had terrible days and could be a thorn in the flesh, but her good days far exceeded her bad. I couldn't bear the thought of my existence without her.

"Aisha needs someone older than you, Masie." Jess took care not to glance at me while she spoke. I wasn't going to let her get away with anything like that.

"And?" I inquired sternly. My wife eventually turned to face me.

"I told Sunny that we weren't looking to adopt, but I'd talk to you about fostering Aisha for a while. She believes that seeing Masie again will benefit the girl."

Everyone in the room was staring at me. Jess's face was flushed with remorse for dumping this on me in front of my family, the kids, and my ex-wife. Masie seemed overjoyed, clearly smitten with Aisha. Surprisingly, it was Jake's look that I most identified with. My three-year-old kid was perplexed.

"It's a tall order." Adrian sent this. She wasn't incorrect, and I realized she was trying to assist, but getting engaged in the argument right then and there would be detrimental to everyone. Surprisingly, the concept instantly helped clear my mind.

"No, I don't want to foster Aisha," I said before anyone else could say anything. "If there's one thing I've learned from our time with Masie, I'm not cut out to be a foster parent. It takes a special kind of person to take in a child, care for it, and then abandon it when the time comes. That is not something I am capable of. It would break my heart to say goodbye to Masie right now."

"But," Jess started. Knowing what I had to do, I cut her off.

"No, it's either foster-to-adopt, as we did with Masie or nothing." I smiled at my wife, knowing that was exactly what she desired. We'd agreed not to adopt any more children at our age, but it was primarily up to me. Masie's enthusiastic squeal from across the table told me what she thought of the scenario.

"Are you certain?" Jess inquired, but she smiled that smile that made me feel warm and fuzzy inside. There was nothing sexual about it, not that Jess didn't have a few grins that could do that when she wanted to.

"Yeah, another college tuition," my brother chuckled. "At the pace you're going; you'll never be able to retire."

"Such is life," I shrugged, then burst out laughing.

"You folks are insane," Adrian said jokingly as she rose and shook her head, but I knew my ex-wife. She meant it entirely. "It's past time we parted ways." Her leaving was unexpected, but I'd given up trying to comprehend my ex's quirks years ago.

"Congratulations," Don remarked as he rose to depart with my ex. They said their last farewells. As they walked out the side gate, I shook my head and then returned to my wife and family.

It was no longer my responsibility to make Adrian happy. I wished Don good luck. It was my responsibility to be there for Jess, and it was a simple task. She was the most pleasing thing that ever happened to me. She and the kids, that is.

"You know, Mother's not incorrect," Bethany said as she resumed the talk. "But, on the other hand, crazy isn't always a terrible thing." I grinned, thinking that it wasn't the first time my older daughter had gotten the better of my ex and me.

"You're never going to make it, old guy!" Neil made a joke.

"You'd best pray I don't," I snarled. "Because if I die too soon, you and Bethany will have another mouth to feed."

In the will we made when our son was born, we left Jake to my daughter Bethany and Neil. We were too old to put it off any longer, so why wait? When Masie entered the picture, we added her. It was probably time for another upgrade.

"No issue," my son-in-law said, laughing.

"Just slow down a bit," Bethany said. "At the pace you're going; we'll need a palace to accommodate all your two babies!"

"Don't be concerned," Jess interrupted. "I want to live a very long time."

"How about my brother?" Tommy inquired, his smirk still on his face.

"He wouldn't dare die before me," Jess responded almost solemnly. "Not after having me wait for him for so long."

"There's that," my sister said, laughing.

"Do you understand what this means?" Jess questioned me directly.

"No more steak for daddy," Masie exclaimed, making everyone laugh as she came into my lap and hugged me. Jake clamored out of his chair and leaped on me from it, just missing the family jewels.

"It's simple, tiger!" I resituated him with a snort.

"You'll like Aisha, Daddy," Masie said enthusiastically. "She's humorous, and she has a dark complexion. She doesn't have to be concerned about getting sunburned!"

"I'm sure your mother is overjoyed," I couldn't help but remark.

"Just for that, smartass," Jess remarked, a smirk on her face. "You get to reapply Masie's sunblock. And while you're at it, you may as well do Jake."

"Yes, sweetheart," I said. That got me a kiss.

"So much for no PDA," my niece Sarah said. She was also constantly texting. I'm sure she informed her sister about everything she hadn't seen.

"That was almost usually the case with these two. They're unconvinced." Tommy was smiling despite, or maybe because of, his remarks.

"Like you're any better," his wife snidely said.

"A good point!" he responded as he reached for Emily. She made a feeble attempt to flee.

As they kissed, my sister whispered, "I miss Bob."

"I need a partner," my niece continued, her voice depressed.

"Funny you should mention it," Jess said, his gaze fixed on Sarah. "I've got a nephew..."

I shook my head and shut out the remainder of the chat. I knew whose nephew she was referring to, and he was a friendly kid, but I was not going to become involved in one of my wife's match-making scams. Instead, I returned my attention to the still seated children on my lap.

"Would you two mind going with me to find the apple pie Mom made?" I spoke it quietly so that only they could hear it. They both smiled broadly. Everyone was so preoccupied with Jess and Sarah that they failed to notice. Masie slid off my lap, and I took a step back, holding Jake in my arms. My youngest daughter clasped my hand in hers as we made our way toward the home.

"And where are the three of you going?" Tommy inquired, appearing abruptly behind us with Junior in tow.

"Jess, you heard me. I need to apply sunscreen to the youngsters." It was an excellent response, but Tommy knew too much about me.

"And steal some apple pie," he countered. I didn't bother disputing it, especially since the youngsters were thrilled.

"Are you certain you want to accompany us inside? It seems like Jess is arranging a date for your kid with some odd man. You don't want to..."

"Please!" sneered my older brother. "Sarah has a decent head on her shoulders and is capable of selecting her partner. Emily is also present. She has a much harder audience than I do. Besides, Jess will not hook Emily up with a loser."

"There's that," I acknowledged, leading the way inside with a groan. "I hope no one else desires apple pie. There will be nothing left of this group."

"We'll reduce it in half," Masie remarked, her voice remarkably authoritative. "This way, there will be plenty for everyone."

"Spoilsport!" Tommy sighed. "You sound eerily similar to your mum!" Masie's face lit up, and I couldn't stop giggling.

******

The early morning light streamed in through the bedroom window. Jess was still sleeping and snoring softly. I smiled down at her, wanting to wake her but knew she needed the rest. I opted for turning her over, so she was on my shoulder. Jess roused slightly before nuzzling deeper and falling asleep again. I smiled, kissed the top of her head, and then softly ruffled her hair.

It had been a hectic week, but most weeks were like this. The kids were growing and demanding more and more attention, which Jess and I had no issue providing them. They were all excellent children.

I'm not sure how long I laid there, relishing the feel of Jess against me and letting my thoughts wander, but my wife soon awoke. She raised her head, glanced at me, and slowly smiled. I kissed her with my head down. Jess answered with more zeal than I had anticipated, which was OK with me.

"What was it for?" I wondered afterward.

"Well, it's your birthday, after all." When Jess awoke like this, she was attractive as heck.

"Good argument," I said, laying over her and making her giggle.

"Aren't we a touch too old for this?" She made a joke. "I mean, you're sixty years old today!"

"Yes, I am," I said, gazing down at my wife and showing her my love and want. "Would you want to know what I was thinking just before you awoke?"

"Sure." Jess slid her fingers between us and gripped my tenseness. She was obviously in a good mood. It took me a while to recall what I was saying.

"I was thinking about my fiftieth birthday. It was the last one I had before you re-entered my life."

"And?" she said when I had finished speaking. Concentration was difficult, mainly when Jess put her hand inside my pajamas.

"I remember feeling so ancient at the time," I said, hoping she would get it. "But it's been nine years, and I don't feel quite as old as then. That is what having you in my life has done for me. It's made me feel young again... well, not so much young as alive. Do you follow me?"

"Yes," she said, sexily smiling. "I adore you as well." We exchanged passionate kisses. It was intense, but Jess backed away too fast for my taste. I realized what she meant when she said, "We'll have to move quickly. The kids will be awakened shortly. They are ecstatic about your birthday."

We got rid of the garments between us at a particular time. I wanted to take my time and ensure that whatever came next was done correctly. I began kissing my wife's body, but Jess giggled and drew my lips back to hers.

"They'll have plenty of time for that once everyone has gone to bed tonight. Right now, we must act rapidly!" Jess grasped my rigidity and drew it to her core. She massaged me down the length of her entrance. It was moist and inviting. "Besides, I'm prepared. You, too, are!" To illustrate her point, she squeezed my cock.

With one long, leisurely thrust, I pushed inside my nine-year-old wife. The whole time, Jess whimpered. My arms were outstretched, my hands resting on each side of her head on the bed. I studied her face as I sought to instill fire deep inside her. Jess threw her arms around my arms and clung on as I accelerated. It didn't take long for me to throw all I had at her.

"Come in, me!" my wife said as we got closer. "I'd want to feel it!" We were over the concern of her being pregnant, but it didn't stop Jess from wanting to feel me fill her. I was delighted to help.

"Soon!" I grumbled, resisting my release for as long as I could. Jess' response was to wrap her legs around my thighs and pull me in a while, raising her hips off the bed. When I felt her claws drive deep into my arms, I snapped. "Now!"

"Yes!" Jess sobbed as we collided for the last time. I lost track of almost everything except the sensation of my come filling my wife and Jess's body trembling under me in relief.

"Now that's how you start a new decade," I grumbled as I collapsed into the bed, tired.

"Just keep it in mind for next year, when it's my time."

"Oh, I will," I said, laughing. Jess's upper lip was sweaty, and I couldn't stop kissing it. She opened her lips to mine and accepted my kisses without resentment until I began touching her chest.

"Later," she replied as she pushed my hands away and rolled out of bed. "We need to get started. It's going to be an eventful day." Jess grabbed for her clothing and started to re-dress.

"What exactly does it mean?" I inquired, getting out of bed and doing the same thing. "I informed everyone that I didn't want to go to a party."

"Do you have no idea who your family is?" Jess snorted.

"Wonderful," I sighed. I didn't want to go to the party, but visiting my family was never terrible.

Jess had barely finished buttoning her pajama top by the time I put mine on. I'd never bothered to unbutton them in the first place. It was too much for me to see how lovely she looked with her breasts popping out. I grabbed Jess and slid into bed.

She resisted me, but not very hard. We both began laughing sometime near the middle, which barely lasted till the door was knocked on. Jess pushed herself away from me and struggled to arrange her pajamas.

She also focused on buttoning them up. I moved my weight to sit up and lean against the headboard.

"Please come in!" Jess squeaked when I phoned. When she noticed me beaming, she gave me a stern look.

My three angels appeared as the door opened. Masie was a sixteen-year-old beauty bringing a plate of what smelled like my favorite breakfast. Jake was eight years old and, despite having had a shower the night before, he was already filthy. He was just like my son. He was holding an orange juice bottle as well as the syrup.

"Happy birthday!" they said, kissing me on the cheek.

Aisha was practically a teenager and seemed to be equally as lovely as her elder sister but differently. Her complexion was more dark than brown, and she had one of those wide-open grins that could light up a whole room. She also had long black hair that she liked to wear in cornrows and braids. Jess and Masie were both specialists in dealing with it.

Aisha was carrying nothing except the family iPad. When I saw my eldest daughter's face on the TV, I smiled. They'd FaceTimed Bethany to ensure she could participate. It made me happy to know they wanted to involve her.

Bethany said, "Happy birthday, Dad." When the screen switched to Neil and his three children, I was ready to react. "Congratulations on your birthday, Grandpa!"

"Thank you very much." The following few minutes were hectic as the kids crawled into bed with Jess and me as the grandchildren sang an inferior version of Happy Birthday, headed by Neil, whose voice was the worst of them all. I wasn't delighted when Jess and my kids joined in, but I handled it as gracefully as possible.

"All right, we've got to leave," Bethany remarked afterward. "We've got a lot planned for later today. Have a wonderful day!"

"Plans?" When I inquired, my eldest daughter merely laughed and disconnected.

"How large is this celebration going to be?" I questioned Jess, but Masie interrupted her before she could respond.

"Which party? There will be no celebration." She gave me a restraining gaze as if she'd learned from the finest. Right then and there, she and her mother might have been broken. It didn't take a genius to figure out that the younger kids were looking forward to surprising me and that neither my wife nor Masie wanted me to spoil their surprise.

"Why aren't we eating?" Distracting Aisha and Jake, Jess proposed.

Jake agreed and dove into the mound of bacon they'd cooked. Aisha paused but then followed suit. We were soon all choosing from the plates on the tray. There was much taunting and joking amongst the three kids, and Jess and I weren't much better. I argued that my wife had been the first to throw food, but she denied it. The bedding needed to be changed by the time we were through, but that was OK. You only turn sixty once in your life.

"Okay, it's time for your father to go into the shower and get ready. The birthday kid is in for a big day." Jess smiled because she knew how much I despised events in my honor. I couldn't let her enjoy my misery any longer, so I went down and kissed her before placing my lips near her ear.

"You pressed the wrong button," I said quietly. When she realized I was correct, Jess instantly looked down and flushed. Not only did she forget a button, but in her rush to get dressed, all the buttons above it were off by one.

"How come you didn't tell me sooner?"

"Can I tell you anything, Mom?" Jake inquired, his face puzzled. Jess's flush darkened even more.

"How much I adore her," I interrupted as solemnly. "Of certainly," she says.

"That's ridiculous," Jack said. "You say it all the time."

"He tells us all that," Aisha said a wide grin on her face.

"Well, it's true," I said with a shrug.

"We're aware." Masie's grin was as broad as Aisha's but slightly slower to emerge. "And we adore you as well." She turned to face the younger two children and said, "Let's get started. We still have to wrap Dad's gift."

I observed as the youngsters filed out of the room. Masie was the last to go. She returned her gaze just as she was about to go out the door. "By the way, Mom, your shirt isn't properly buttoned." She stated it straight-faced, but I could see the amusement in her eyes.

"Oh my, I must have been wary when I put it on last night. Thanks." Jess had quick thinking, but it was probably wasted on Masie.

"After Dad's done, you may as well take a shower. I'll keep Aisha and Jake entertained for the next hour until it's time for us to go."

"Where are you going?" I inquired, knowing she would not respond. Masie smiled as she snuck out of the room. As soon as we were alone, I turned to Jess. "Did our little child just give us some 'alone time?'"

"Not at all," she moaned. "She'll be able to drive in a few months."

"Perhaps it's time we have the conversation with her?" I thought it was a brilliant idea, but Jess' astonished expression made me reconsider. Masie was a lovely young lady, and I wasn't blind to the guys who had begun sniffing about lately. "I mean, she's sixteen years old and..."

"Men!" Jess chimed in with a deep sigh. "You're a touch out of step with the times, sweetheart. I had that conversation with her years ago."

"Did you?" I inquired, surprised. "Did everything go well?"

"Fine." I didn't like it when Jess gave me a one-word response, but it could be for the best in this situation. Nonetheless, I needed to be present for my children.

"Is there anything I should be aware of?" Jess smiled, leaned in, and kissed me in response to my query.

"Masie, on the other hand, has a good head on her shoulders. Plus, she's not in any hurry to become serious with a male."

"That's great to hear," I answered really. "However, because you had a chat so long ago, maybe we should..."

"I check in with her now and then," Jess said. "Besides, she speaks about males with Bethany. I suppose it's simpler since Masie considers herself her elder sister, despite the age gap. Bethany doesn't get into specifics with me, but she keeps me updated on what I need to know."

"And who is meant to keep me up to date?"

"Me," my wife said, laughing.

"And yet," I pointed out, "I had no idea you'd already had 'the conversation' with her." Jess didn't appear upset by my outburst. "Will you let me know when she begins dating?" My wife almost rolled her eyes at me. "I'm talking about dating someone seriously. I know she's had a couple of boyfriends already."

"Of certainly," she says. "We need to speak about putting her on birth control soon," Jess said after a pause.

"Already? She hasn't even found a steady lover." I blanched a little at the prospect, but it's not like I hadn't faced it before. "Bethany didn't start until she had her first serious boyfriend," she says.

"Who do you suppose recommended we begin with Macie now?" Jess inquired. "Furthermore, the best time to begin birth control is before she has a significant relationship. The challenge is to find a method to do it without giving her the impression that you approve of her having sex previously."

"I suppose I preferred it when you kept me in the dark."
I was just half-joking. Certain aspects of parenting
remained difficult no matter how many children you
had.

"I reasoned. Why do you suppose I never informed you
about my conversation with her?" This time, Jess
laughed at me. She also selected that time to begin
mending her buttons.

"You know, Masie did say she'd keep the other kids
entertained for an hour." I grabbed my wife's hand.
"It's also my birthday." Jess shook her head but sprang
into my arms. I began unbuttoning the shirt she'd just
mended when she grabbed my hand and pulled me
back.

"I'm not going back into that bed until the sheets have
been changed! Someone thought it would be good to
have a food battle."

"Well," I murmured, a gradual grin on my face. "Masie did propose that you shower after I did. We could always save water and go on a hike together?"

"Yes, there is that." My wife smiled and let go of my hand, allowing me to finish undressing her. "After all, it is your birthday today, as you seem eager to remind me." Jess reached out to assist me in getting out of my clothing. It didn't take long for us to be nude.

Over the previous nine years, I'd gotten to know my wife's body rather well, and it never stopped to astonish me. It may have thickened with time, but it still got to me in all the right places. It felt amazing when she came into my arms and snuggled against me while we kissed.

"I'm getting poked," she joked as she drew away from me and held my hardness in her palm. She caressed it a few times before releasing it and walking into the restroom. "A shower was promised to me." Jess glanced over her shoulder at me in the most enticing manner possible.

"You were," I chuckled. "I'll be there in a second."

I rushed to the bed and removed the linens. I also took the spare set from the closet. I placed the fitted sheet on first, then the flat sheet. As I walked toward the restroom, I believed that was plenty.

It occurred to me that what I'd said to Jess earlier was correct. It wasn't so much that having her in my life made me feel youthful as it did alive. I was happier at sixty with Jess than I'd ever been. That made the number of years I'd lived nearly insignificant. Not that I didn't want as many more dates with her as I could get.

"Perhaps I'll cut down on the red meat."

"I heard you!" Jess sobbed in the shower. I snorted and burst out laughing.

"Maybe!" I responded. As I entered the steamy bathroom, I replied. Jess like her showers to be hot. I pulled the glass door wide, taking in the sight of her gleaming physique. "Congratulations on your birthday!" Jess burst out laughing as she embraced me with wide arms.

"I think I'm meant to be the one saying that." I took a step back from our embrace and examined her whole physique.

"Being able to see you like this is the finest birthday gift ever."

"You must adore me," Jess laughed, before becoming serious and adding, "And I adore you." The presence of you in my life has made all the difference." We kissed softly and intensely for quite some time before she took a step back. "Now, in terms of birthday gifts..." I moaned in anticipation. However, I didn't have to wait long for what happened next.

I'd later spend my birthday with my whole family, and despite my complaining, I'd have a good day, but the lady in front of me made it all worthwhile.

Life was amusing. It had taken Jess and myself a quarter-century to rediscover one other. Some days I regretted it, but then I thought about what would have occurred if we hadn't found one other again. I'd also consider what life would be like without Bethany, Neil, and the kids. That wasn't something I wanted to think about for very long. Not to add, if things had gone differently, Masie, Aisha, and even Jake would not have been in our life. That was incomprehensible.

Life was amusing, but I felt that everything had a way of turning out the way it was intended to, or maybe I was just fortunate. Even if I had made a different decision when I was younger, there was no guarantee that Jess and I would have gotten along. We had always loved one other, but maybe we needed the time apart to comprehend it properly. Perhaps not, but the point was that we were now together, which was all that mattered. There would be no more squandered time when it came to Jess and me.

CPSIA information can be obtained
at www.ICGtesting.com
Printed in the USA
LVHW080756050522
717841LV00007B/329